MW01235330

Dearest Pal

DONNA McCALL McWATERS

authorHOUSE®

AuthorHouse™
1663 Liberty Drive, Suite 200
Bloomington, IN 47403
www.authorhouse.com
Phone: 1-800-839-8640

First published by AuthorHouse 10/2/2008

ISBN: 978-1-4389-0867-0 (sc)

Library of Congress Control Number: 2008907301

Printed in the United States of America
Bloomington, Indiana

This is a work of fiction.
This book is printed on acid-free paper.

To the memory of Janice who inspired
us all in ways she never realized.

Table of Contents

Dearest Pal

Prologue

The morning sun streamed through the window and illuminated the dust particles floating in the air. The house, deserted by its inhabitants, settled into a quiet emptiness as the steady tick of the clock magnified the lonely stillness throughout. Janet, relieved in the rare gift of solitude, settled into her favorite chair and heaved a sigh of relief. Silence permeated the room and her thoughts wandered back to another time. She thought of the antique cedar box hidden deep in the back of the closet. She rose from her chair, walked to the closet, and opened the door. She reached for the short stool in the corner and stood upon it. Janet stretched her arm deep inside the top shelf of the closet until she felt the outline of the cedar box and secured it in her arms. Seated once again in the chair, she placed it in her lap and opened the lid. A faint musty smell escaped the box and the yellowed letters lay before her. Quite early in life, Janet had suffered the loss of her mother and grew up alone in the care of her maternal grandparents. She had never known her father and his whereabouts remained a mystery. The antique cedar box came into her possession upon her mother's death and contained all she knew about him. She never shared the letters or revealed their existence to anyone but kept them a secret as if by doing so she might hold their message captive forever. She often sensed the presence of both parents around her as she read the yellowed letters over and over devouring them with both joy and sadness.

Janet reached inside the box and lifted the letters out and held them close to her cheek for a time as if embracing an old friend. She untied the blue ribbon that bound them and slipped the first letter from its envelope as a few pieces of the brittle paper fell into her lap. Her eyes traveled to the top corner of the letter and the familiar words *Leslie, South Carolina, Tuesday morning, August 22, 1934. Dearest Pal....*

Part 1
Courtship

Chapter 1

Nineteen thirty-four proved a hard year for most families. The country, in a depression since nineteen twenty-nine, offered few jobs or opportunities. Weary in its struggle, the country looked to government for a respite from its troubles. In the small textile towns in the South, countless families eked out a living and prayed for better times. Virginia Dare Nivens was a member of such a family.

Virginia roused early from her sleep on this August morning in 1934. The day broke hot and humid. The temperature in the room, already oppressive, gave an uncomfortable preview of the day ahead. A faint fragrance of honeysuckle drifted through the open window. Virginia's mind wandered back in time to the previous summer and the church picnic, the church picnic where Bill first approached her, his sky blue eyes dancing and a sheepish grin on his face. She found herself lonely for the man who had been by her side for over a year and thought about the letter in the cedar box on her dresser. Virginia sprang from the bed. She retrieved the letter and caressed the familiar writing with her eyes.

Leslie, South Carolina
Tuesday morning
August 22, 1934

Dearest Pal,

I wonder how you are. I came upon some bad luck since I left. I traveled on the train from Clover to York and from there to Rock Hill yesterday. I spent the night in Rock Hill and let the train leave me this morning. I'll be back in a couple of weeks. I hope to get a long letter from you. I am writing this letter from the filling station where we stopped to get out of the rain the last time we were together. I am listening to Fred Kirby and Moon Light and Skies. Talk about having the blues, I have them. I woke this morning with blues all around my bed. You can mail my letter on to Kershaw. I'll get there sometime today. I would write more but I must go now. I'll write more next time.

So long Pal,
Bill

Virginia heard the sound of her mother's voice and quickly folded the letter and slid it back in the box.

"If only Bill could find work here," She thought. "Things might be different then."

All she could do now was wait and hope for better days. After all, two weeks wasn't such a long time.

The kitchen table was clear of dishes as Virginia entered the room.

"Virginia, you're late this morning and we finished our breakfast long ago. I left some on the stove for you," her mother said. "Hurry up though. I have a lot to do and I want out of this kitchen before the day gets any hotter."

"I won't be long," replied Virginia. "If you'll leave the dishes, I'll finish up here."

"Your sister and I are gathering the clothes for the wash woman. You didn't forget that today is wash day did you?" Virginia's mother continued without waiting for an answer. "We'll be in the yard starting the fire for her," she continued. "Come on out when you finish here. We'll need some help."

Virginia enjoyed Bertha, the tall Negro wash woman with the wide-toothed grin. She enjoyed the bantering and teasing that Bertha quite often engaged in. Her jovial countenance belied the true nature of her life, a life spent in a continual struggle to raise several small children alone. Bertha and her husband had never realized biological children of their own and after his death Bertha took in orphaned children to combat her loneliness. She was a strong woman who never complained of her hardships.

Virginia hated the thought of the round, black pot with its boiling water. The day was hot enough and the large oak tree under which the pot sat offered little relief from the summer heat. It often took most of a day to boil the clothes, rinse them and hang them to dry. She banished the thought from her mind and walked over to the wood stove to retrieve the plate of food left for her by her mother. She sat alone at the table and picked at the food. The sultry morning heat had robbed her of any appetite. Thoughts of the sudden summer shower a few days before filled her mind. She and Bill had taken refuge under the canopy of a filling station by the side of the road. Enticed by a grove of trees surrounding the lake at the end of the road, they started on a journey down the hot, dusty road. The lake promised an ideal location for a picnic and swim, but most of all, private time alone. She smiled at the memory of running through the rain to the old filling station, clothes dripping wet, and panting for breath.

The familiar sound of Bertha's laughter interrupted Virginia's thoughts. She walked to the window and saw steam rise from the pot as Bertha slowly dropped the clothes into the boiling water. She picked up a long stick and shoved all the clothes under the water. Her laughter filled the air as she teased with Virginia's younger sister, Catherine, and her mother. The two gold front teeth that Bertha was most proud of glistened in her wide toothed grin.

"Where's Miss Virginia this morning?" Bertha asked. "Surely that child's not still in the bed. Not sick is she?"

"Oh, no," Virginia's mother answered. "She's just slow moving this morning. She'll join us directly."

"We sure can use her help today," Bertha answered "Sure can use her help today."

Virginia washed the remainder of the dishes and joined the trio in the yard. The hot day stretched long before them.

The temperature continued to climb throughout the morning and shortly after lunch the heat forced the trio inside. Bertha sipped on a glass of iced tea in the kitchen and wiped the sweat from her brow with a red bandana from her apron pocket.

"Hope we don't get a storm this afternoon," she said. "That one a couple days ago liked to scared me to death. All my children were running and yelling. I almost never got them to stop. There wasn't any calming them down until that storm was over. No sir, not until that thunder stopped."

"I don't think we'll get any rain today," replied Virginia's mother. We can sure use some though."

Bertha rose from her chair and placed her empty glass in the sink. "Sure do appreciate the tea, Mrs. Nivens. Guess I better be going now," she said. "Be back next week though."

Virginia's mother slipped some money into Bertha's apron and the screen door slammed as she made her exit. The day had just begun for her. She had many more clothes to wash before she would know any relief from this day.

Virginia left the hot kitchen and stretched out on the bed in her room. She fanned herself with a paper fan. Her dark hair hung limp around her face and the paper fan offered little relief from the heat. Asthma had plagued Virginia since early childhood and was not a stranger to her entire family. Passed down from her father's side of the family, only a few family members had escaped its ravages. Virginia was not one of them and often found herself confined to bed as a result. Today, her breathing was labored and the stifling heat only added to her plight. She reached for the glass of water from the bedside table and swallowed two of the yellow pills the doctor prescribed. She then picked up a writing tablet and pencil, plumped the pillow behind her on the bed and composed a letter to Bill.

Virginia remained confined to bed for a few days and was then able to resume her daily activities. She was anxious for some word from Bill. Bill moved around a lot depending on each job he found and its duration. It was possible that her last letter to him simply hadn't caught up with him or maybe his present job offered no time to correspond with her. Even so, the waiting seemed long indeed. She heard her mother as she moved from room to room throughout the house in her daily effort to keep the house tidy and neat.

Virginia called to her from her bedroom. "Mother, has the mail come yet?"

"Not yet, but it shouldn't be much longer. The mailman's already late," she answered. "What is it you're waiting for?"

"Oh nothing," Virginia answered.

"Hope its not some news from that Blackmon boy you're so fond of. You know how your father and I feel about that," her mother replied.

"Oh, mother," Virginia answered. "I don't know what's so wrong with Bill. It's not his fault there was a depression. A lot of men are out of work. Why, even Daddy was out of work for a while. Bill's trying as hard as he can to find steady work."

"I don't know, Virginia. There's something about that boy that puzzles me," her mother said. "I don't quite know what it is but there's something all right."

"It's just because he's not from around here and you don't know his family at least three generations back," Virginia answered.

"Virginia, better listen to your Daddy and me. Now quit wasting time and help me in this house. There's enough to do to keep six people busy."

Virginia joined her mother and shared in the dreaded housework that never seemed to end all the while keeping a close eye on the front screen door for the mailman due to arrive shortly.

"I don't know what's so wrong with Bill," she thought. "They just don't know him like I do."

Virginia's younger sister, Catherine, joined her and her mother and the three of them endured the housework together. About lunchtime Virginia heard the footsteps of the mailman and the rattle of the mailbox as he dropped the mail in. She crossed her fingers for luck and hurried to the front door.

"How are you Mr. Parks?" she inquired of the mailman as he stepped off the porch.

"Oh, hello, Virginia," he turned to reply. "I'm fine. Sure would be nice if the temperature would spare us some though. This is the hottest summer I can remember in a while," he continued. "Are you waiting for something special today?"

"No Mr. Parks, I'm just trying to help mother. It saves her time if I bring the mail in," Virginia answered.

Mr. Parks smiled and continued down the walk. Not much slipped by him and he had already noticed the letter with the out of town postmark delivered to her the previous week. He would keep an eye on that.

The screen door slammed as Virginia entered the house. She dropped the mail on a table in the hall and hurried to her room. She locked the door and clutched the letter to her heart. The postmark read: Anderson, South Carolina, August 29, 11 A.M., 1934. Virginia opened the envelope and began to read.

Anderson, South Carolina
Tuesday, P.M.

Dearest Virginia,

I received your letter this morning. I did not have time to get this letter off on the train so don't be surprised at it being late. I sure was glad to hear from you. I am very sorry to hear that you have been in bed. It hurts to know that my only pal, my sweetest pal, is sick in bed. I would rather be there myself. Guess you are better by now. If you had told me sooner I would have been there some way. I will be with you on Friday if nothing happens. If I am not there on Friday, look for me on Saturday.

I watch the moon every night too, Virginia. It sure has been beautiful hasn't it? It would do a lot of good if I could see you but it won't be as long as it has been.

By now you are holding the tiny wooden cross I made for you. I put the handwork on it myself. I don't know whether you will like it or not but I was thinking of you when I made it. I made myself one. I wouldn't take a five dollar bill for it.

Well, I will close for now. Don't worry and don't be sick.

Till we meet again,
Your, Bill

Virginia reread the letter twice and placed it back inside the envelope. She gazed at the tiny wooden cross in her hand and traced the outline of its delicate handwork with her fingers. She walked over to the dresser, fumbled in her jewelry box for the fragile gold chain she saved for special occasions, and slipped it through the round opening in the top of the cross. She glanced in the mirror, softly caressed the necklace, and dropped it inside the collar of her blouse, seeing no need to draw attention to it at this time.

Chapter 2

September slipped in and carried with it more hot, steamy weather. The new month found Virginia and Catherine in the kitchen preparing food for the annual church picnic. The air in the kitchen hung heavy with the aroma of ham biscuits and fried chicken already placed in straw baskets lined in a row across the kitchen table. Bertha had labored all morning over the white tablecloths that now lay neatly folded in the wicker basket by the door. Virginia walked to the table and lifted the lid on one of the baskets. She carefully slid canned peaches and strawberry jam alongside the chicken and ham biscuits. The kitchen was uncomfortable in the summer heat and she stopped long enough to tie her dark hair back with a blue ribbon. Her thoughts transported her to the old oak tree that dominated the front yard of the church, its large branches a promise of cool comfort. It was Virginia's and Catherine's duty to drape the white tablecloths over the rock wall that embraced the cemetery like sheltering stone arms. Only then were they allowed to join their friends under the old oak. Virginia wondered how many before her had found relief from the summer heat under its shady canopy or how many romances had ignited beneath the branches of the ancient tree. She looked forward to an afternoon of idle chatter with her friends. One year had slipped by since she met Bill at this same picnic. In hard times, it was not uncommon for young men to travel from town to town in search of steady employment and Bill Blackmon found himself in this position in 1934. Bill traveled to Clover on the train, landed a job in the Hawthorne Mill, one of the local textile mills, and planned to remain until the work ran out. He rented a room in the boardinghouse downtown and paid on a daily basis. Virginia's cousin, Daniel also worked in the Hawthorne and he and Bill became fast friends. It was with Daniel that Bill arrived at the church picnic. Virginia noticed him at once but pretended not to. She watched as Daniel introduced him to all their friends and smiled as they walked toward her.

"Virginia, this is Bill Blackmon," Daniel said. "He's new here and works with me in the mill. He's a pretty good sort though."

Virginia smiled and replied, "Nice to meet you Bill."

Bill nodded his head as he and Daniel sat down beside her on the blanket. His blue eyes complimented the summer sky.

The quilted blankets spread under the old, oak tree created a kaleidoscope of color as Virginia and her family arrived at the church. Some of her friends playfully teased one another and their laughter carried through the air and caught her ears as she and her sister helped to unload the car of its edible cargo. They retrieved the folded tablecloths and hurriedly draped them over the stone wall as several women carried dishes of food and sat them all along the pristine, white tablecloths.

"Whitest tablecloths I've ever seen," commented Mrs. Essie Boyd.

"Bertha would be proud to hear that," Virginia couldn't help but think.

A warm breeze teased the edges of the tablecloths and the mummer of happy voices and laughter drifted through the churchyard. Virginia joined her friends under the ancient oak and was delightfully enveloped in their light hearted chatter.

The following Friday Bill rode the train from Anderson to Clover.

The radio playing Ray Benson's, *Goodnight Sweetheart,* only added to the melancholy mood Virginia found herself in. The fun of the picnic had dissipated and left Virginia sad in its going. She longed to hear from Bill as she searched the radio for a different song to lift the melancholy mood she drowned in. Catherine joined her in the bedroom and they listened to the radio together. It pleased Virginia to claim her company this night.

A light tap on the door interrupted them and Virginia opened the door.

"Someone's here to see you," her mother said just as Virginia caught the stern look on her mother's face. "Don't forget what I told you about that boy, Virginia," her mother admonished as she turned and walked away.

"It's Bill. It must be Bill," Virginia thought.

"Don't forget what mother told you about that boy," her sister teased and disappeared down the hall.

Virginia flew to the door and stepped onto the porch to greet Bill.

Bill rented a room downtown and the weekend raced by. Neither the cool reception by Virginia's mother or her watchful eye dampened their time together. Bill's travels had served to make him a more knowledgeable and mature individual without the destruction of any youthful charm. Virginia found these qualities irresistible and so lacking in the boys she was accustomed to. She hung on his every word as the hours flew by.

On Sunday afternoon, Bill caught the train to Lancaster. At the depot Virginia watched the train depart until it became a long iron snake in the distance.

She stood transfixed until her sister broke the silence and said, "Virginia, let's go. Mother will come looking for us if we don't."

Virginia heaved a long sigh and turned toward her sister.

"Maybe Bill will stay next time," she said.

"Maybe so," Catherine answered.

Virginia and her sister arrived home just in time for the evening prayer service at church. Virginia slipped into her coolest summer dress and brushed her hair. She left the delicate wooden cross around her neck in plain view.

"Guess I might as well face the music now," she thought. "Mother will find out sooner or later. It might as well be sooner."

Virginia sat with Catherine and a few friends in the back row of the church. It didn't take long before the church filled with the hushed whispers of its congregation. The sounds of the hymn, *Come Thou Almighty King,* rang out in affirmation that the service was to begin shortly. All eyes turned to the front of the church as Reverend Asa Hambright entered the pulpit. Mrs. Rosa Kirk pounded out the hymn, *The Church in the Wildwood,* and everyone rose to sing.

Reverend Hambright lost no time in getting into the sermon. His deep baritone voice rose and fell like the rumble of thunder before a summer storm and allowed no diversions from its message. With beads of perspiration dripping from his face, he held his audience captive for forty five minutes. Mrs. Addie Mae Frie, the choir director, rose on cue from Rev. Jones and stood in front of the choir. Several members in the congregation requested hymns, most of them the familiar hymns of their youth, *The Old Rugged Cross, What a Friend We Have in Jesus,* or *Bringing in the Sheaves.* The chords of the piano rang out and the church sprang alive in loud praise. During the last chorus of *Bringing in the Sheaves,* Virginia detected the faint odor of smoke. She glanced over at Catherine and realized by the puzzled look on her face that she wasn't the only one. Several members stopped singing and others soon followed. Row by row, silence permeated the church.

"The church is on fire!" "The church is on fire!" someone shouted from several rows in front of Virginia.

"Everyone get out!" Reverend Hambright shouted.

"Oh, dear, oh dear," Mrs. Addie Mae whined as Reverend Hambright grabbed her by the arm to lead her out of the burning church.

The smoke continued to snake under the choir room door and several members stumbled out into the night coughing and gasping. The fire shed its fiery glow on the faces of the startled church members as they stood and watched.

Several men filled buckets of water from the well behind the church. The fire hissed like an angry cat as the water struck but continued to rage on. There was nothing to do except wait for the fire truck. The wail of the fire whistle echoed again and again into the still night.

Mrs. Addie Mae broke into loud sobs.

"Oh what will we do now?" she sobbed over and over.

Mrs. Addie Mae's husband, Norman, walked over and put his arm around her.

"Now Addie Mae, no need for you to work yourself up so. Everything is all right," he said.

Virginia's mother walked over and took Mrs. Addie Mae by the arm and walked her to the car. The fire illuminated both of them as they sat staring out from the car window, wet tears streaming down Mrs. Addie Mae's face.

"Mrs. Addie Mae doesn't need to be here," Mrs. Reevie Sizemore said. "She has a bad heart, you know."

Several women nodded in agreement never taking their eyes from the angry fire that now licked at the sky like a wild dragon.

Virginia gathered with her friends under the old, oak and waited with the rest. She heard the deep heavy rumble of the fire truck in the distance and stood mesmerized by the fire as it sped across the churchyard. When the lights from the truck captured the field behind the church, two lone figures stood out in the night darkness. Virginia recognized them as the Dalton brothers Clyde and Lyle.

Chapter 3

The fire at the church monopolized all conversation at the breakfast table the following Monday morning. Virginia glanced at her father as he finished the strong black cups of coffee he favored each morning.

"You girls help your mother today," he admonished as he rose from the table. "She has enough to do today to keep several people busy."

"We will," Catherine answered.

"No time to daydream today, Virginia," he continued.

"I know, Daddy," Virginia answered with a long sigh.

Virginia realized what a long hard day at the Hawthorne awaited him as she watched him retrieve his gray felt hat from a hook on the wall.

"Bye Daddy," she said as he left the room.

Virginia yawned as she sat at the table. She and Catherine had talked well into the night about the fire. She wondered if anyone else had noticed the Dalton brothers standing in the field behind the church. She couldn't shake the feeling that they might in some way be responsible for the fire. But she hadn't mentioned this to anyone.

"Mother, how do you think the fire started?" she asked.

"Too soon to tell yet," her mother answered. "Sure is a shame though. With times as hard as these it might be a while before we can rebuild." She heaved a sigh and continued, "Guess we'll make do somehow."

"Maybe it's not as bad as it looked last night," Catherine chimed in.

"Time will tell," replied her mother.

"Mother," Virginia said. "I heard from Ailene Boatwright last night that Mr. Oren Stroupe needs some help in his dime store downtown. "It won't pay much but it will help out some. What do you think?"

"Now, Virginia, you know your health isn't that good with your asthma and all. What about the days you might miss because of it?" her mother asked. "Do you think Mr.Oren will understand?"

"I don't know mother, but I can explain it to him and see what he says. It can't hurt to try," Virginia answered.

"I hope you don't get disappointed," her mother replied. "You better get to town and back before the day gets any hotter."

Virginia hurried to her room to dress. Aware that because of her petite size she often appeared much younger, she put on the blue skirt and white blouse that everyone agreed made her look somewhat older. She took the ribbon from her hair and let her dark hair fall in soft curls around her face.

"Are you ready to go?" Virginia called to her sister. "We need to hurry back to help mother."

"Let's go," Catherine replied and appeared in the doorway.

Virginia and Catherine walked to town underneath their father's oversized black umbrella to protect their fair skin from the sun. Virginia tried to calm her nerves as Mr. Oren's dime store came into sight.

"I'll wait outside," her sister said just as they reached the store.

Virginia left Catherine there and took a deep breath before she entered the store to face Mr. Oren.

When Virginia came out of the store, Catherine was engaged in conversation with a handsome young man and she was hesitant to intrude. Instead, she pretended to window shop until the young man walked away. The smile on Virginia's face was visible evidence of success as she approached her sister.

Early the next morning, Virginia walked the familiar sidewalk to Mr. Oren's dime store at ten o'clock and returned at five in the afternoon as she would continue to do every Tuesday and Thursday for the next year.

Over two weeks had slipped by since Virginia bid goodbye to Bill at the train depot. This morning, she found all manner of excuses to hang around on the porch in the hope of the first glimpse of Mr. Parks. She grabbed a broom from the corner and began to sweep the porch. She straightened the cushions on the front porch rockers and watered the tall plant that devoured the entire corner by the door. She had exhausted just about all reasons to dally on the porch, when she heard Mr. Parks whistling as he walked up the street. She noticed him only two doors down and tried hard to resist the temptation to meet him on the sidewalk. Instead, she picked up a magazine from the basket beside the rocker and seated herself on the plump cushion in the rocker. She fumbled through the magazine and waited for Mr. Parks. Virginia rose to greet him, when he turned up the walk toward her.

"Hello Mr. Parks," she said as he stepped onto the porch.

"Oh, hello, Virginia," he replied. "Is this what you're waiting for?"

Mr. Parks held the letter out to her and Virginia blushed as she reached for it.

"Thanks Mr. Parks. "It is," she replied and attempted to hide her embarrassment by brushing at an imaginary spot on her dress.

"Hope your Ma's okay today. It's bad about the fire at the church. Wasn't it?" he continued. "Don't think the damage was as bad as we first figured though."

"That's good Mr. Parks. Mother is fine. Thanks."

Virginia returned to the rocker and scanned the postmark on the letter, unaware as Mr. Parks left the porch and continued back down the walk.

The postmark read: Marion, South Carolina, Tuesday, September 14, 1934. She opened the letter and welcomed Bill's familiar handwriting.

Lancaster, South Carolina
Friday, PM

Dear Virginia,

I guess you will be kind of surprised at getting this late letter but it was the best I could do. I just got home at 12 o'clock today. I had a heck of a time getting home this time, just my luck. I spent several nights in York and the rest in Rock Hill. I caught the freight and came in just a few minutes ago. I am very sorry I couldn't write but you know how it is with me.

Gin, I have a chance at a job here in Lancaster. It is every day work including Sunday. I can make six bucks a week and my board. It's not much but it beats what I've got. I don't know whether you like it or not. I don't because I won't be able to see you as often as I have been. Let me know what you think about it. I don't think I will take it.

I have two or three jobs here to see about. Maybe I can get one to suit me and you. I do want to please you.

Please do not worry while I am away and stay well. I'm looking for a long letter from you. Well, its time for the train.

Forever your,
Bill

Virginia folded the letter and placed it in the envelope. She heard her mother call from inside the house.

"Is there any mail today?" her mother asked.

"There's just a little something for me today. That's all," Virginia answered.

Virginia took the letter to her room, placed it in the cedar box on her dresser and turned the key in the lock. She added the key to the gold chain that held the delicate wooden cross around her neck.

Chapter 4

The hot temperatures of September gave in to the cooler temperatures that precede fall. It proved a relief for Virginia as she walked to and from the dime store. Her struggle with asthma diminished somewhat. She was sick only one day out of the past two weeks and it had not interfered with her work in the dime store. Virginia found the job a respite from the daily grind of endless household chores. The work was uncomplicated and her friends drifted in and out of the tiny store on a daily basis. She considered the job most beneficial to her social life.

One week after the fire, some members of the St. Peter's Methodist Church began repairs on the burned out choir room. Several nights, after the supper meal, Virginia and her family rode to the church to offer their help.

The word in town was that the Dalton brothers started the fire with a lit cigarette. From the age of seven, Clyde and Lyle quite frequently found themselves in trouble. At the age of ten, they broke into the grocery store and relieved the store of several containers of penny candy. Several weeks later they took Mr. Clarence Lattimore's horse, Big George, from the pasture and rode him bareback through the center of the elementary school downtown. They were well known for stealing tobacco to roll cigarettes in the field behind the church. Obviously, Virginia had not been the only one to notice them in the field the night of the fire.

Now, at the age of twelve, the young boys' parents had made arrangements for them to live with an aunt in Morganton, for an undetermined length of time, much to the relief of almost every adult in town.

Bill rode the train to Clover late one Friday afternoon in early September.

In the cooler temperature of late afternoon, Virginia and her family had escaped the stuffy house for the comfortable front porch rockers. Their presence in the rockers enticed several neighbors to join them. Virginia considered all the neighbors in the modest mill houses as family and always missed their visits when the colder temperatures of winter forced them inside. She enjoyed their lively conversations as they competed with one another for the funniest joke or story on each other. In the reflection of the streetlight up the street, Virginia noticed a lone silhouette.

"Who's that coming up the street?" Virginia's mother asked.

"Don't know," her father answered. "He doesn't look familiar to me."

The conversation continued and Virginia kept a close eye on the figure.

"That's Bill," she thought "I just know that's Bill."

Virginia rushed to meet him on the sidewalk and they walked hand in hand toward home. The porch was empty of family and neighbors by the time they arrived and they sat alone in the porch swing until deep into the night as the grandfather clock in the hall chimed away the hours.

Bill had accepted a job in a textile mill in Kershaw that did not require weekend work. The pay was less but a good trade off for free weekends and steady work.

Saturday afternoon, Virginia and Bill walked to the local theater for a matinee. A new movie called *"The Gay Divorce"* starring Ginger Rogers and Fred Astaire was showing and Virginia was crazy to see it. They bumped into some of Virginia's friends inside and joined them later at the local diner, on the corner, in the center of town.

The diner was filled to overflowing with friends by the time Bill and Virginia came through the door. A popular tune of the big band leader, Jimmie Lunceford, rang loudly through the air as they squeezed down the narrow aisle to find a seat in the back. They engaged in intimate conversation until the waitress came to take their order. Daniel and his wife, Anna Jane, appeared and Bill motioned for them to join them.

"How long are you here for this time?" Daniel asked glancing at Bill.

"I'm leaving tomorrow afternoon. I found steady work in Kershaw and I hope to be there for a while at least as long as the mill has work for me," answered Bill.

"You're lucky to have any work right now," said Daniel. "Right now, the Hawthorne is standing three days a week. It's hard on a man with a family. They say with Franklin Roosevelt as president, things should start looking better. They say he'll create enough jobs for all of us. Sure hope its true," Daniel continued.

"That's what I hear," replied Bill. "But you know how those politicians are."

The waitress returned with their order. Bill dropped a coin in the selection box on the table and chose a song for the jukebox.

The tune of *Mood Indigo* slipped in and out of each brief lull in the noise of the busy diner and time slipped by in the midst of all their youthful laughter.

On Sunday morning, Virginia met Bill at St. Peter's Methodist Church and they spent the hour together. Virginia was uncertain as to how Bill, a devout Presbyterian, might receive the small Methodist church. She relaxed, however, as Bill sang the Methodist hymns as if he had heard them all his life. Reverend Hambright delivered an intense sermon that left no opportunity for the mind to wander and Bill glanced over at Virginia each time the Reverend's voice rose and fell. The sun shone through the windows and heated the church to an uncomfortable degree and the end of the sermon came as a pleasant relief. Afterward, Bill and Virginia greeted some friends in the shade of the oak tree in the church yard. Virginia had just introduced Bill to Reverend Hambright, when her eyes caught Daniel and Anna Jane approaching.

"Come and go with us. Anna Jane cooked some chicken and there's plenty for you two," said Daniel.

"Naw, I've got to meet the train before long," Bill replied.

"Aw, come on. We won't let you miss the train. We'll even take you to the depot," Daniel urged and took a few steps toward the car.

Bill and Virginia squeezed into the backseat of the car with Daniel and Anna Jane's two children.

Daniel loaned Bill the car and he and Virginia rode to the lake in the middle of the afternoon. They spread a blanket under a tree and spent their time in quiet conversation. The ducks on the lake paddled to the shore to retrieve the stale bread they tossed and Bill laughed as one duck nibbled at Virginia's finger.

Later in the afternoon, the clouds darkened and thunder grumbled behind them. To beat the ensuing rain, Bill and Virginia returned to Daniel's with only an hour left to catch the train.

"I'll write soon," Bill said as the train left the depot. Stay well and drop me a line."

"I will, Bill," she answered. "I'll write often."

Virginia tried hard to hide her sadness at Bill's departure and mercifully the rain mixed with her tears as she watched the train snake out of sight.

"Maybe he'll stay next time," she thought.

Chapter 5

Virginia returned home and went to her room to write a letter to Bill. She hoped to catch Mr. Parks the next morning and make certain that Bill received the letter by Wednesday. The weekend had slipped by almost without notice and now the thought of the new week dampened Virginia's spirits.

"At least I have my job at the dime store," she thought.

Catherine joined Virginia in the bedroom and attempted to lift her spirits with a few impersonations of Jean Harlow and Mae West, two of the most popular fem fatales of the day. She sensed Virginia's unhappiness at Bill's departure and tried to divert her thoughts to happier things.

"The movie, *The Ghost and Mrs. Muir,* starring Clark Cable and Claudette Colbert is playing at the movie next week. Let's get Mary Lee and Isabelle to go with us to see it next weekend," Catherine said.

"I know. I need a new dress," Virginia replied. "After the movie we could stop by McConnell's and you can help me pick it out. You might find those shoes you want."

"That's what we'll do then," Catherine said.

"I need something to look forward to," Virginia said.

On Tuesday morning, Virginia stopped in front of McConnell's Department store to admire the red coat with the matching beret she first noticed on Friday afternoon. She lingered in front of the store to watch as Mrs. McConnell draped the red coat over the rigid mannequin and plopped the matching plaid beret on its straw blonde wig. The red coat and beret had teased her mind all weekend and she ducked inside long enough to inquire about them. Virginia tried them on and asked Mrs. McConnell to hold them for her. Mrs. McConnell thought for a moment but since Virginia's parents were among some of her best customers, she agreed to on the condition that Virginia pay for the coat and beret before Christmas. Virginia gave Mrs. McConnell some money and sealed the agreement.

"I'll have the coat and beret out before Christmas, Mrs. McConnell," Virginia turned to say as she stood in the doorway.

"I know you will," Mrs. McConnell replied with a smile on her face. "I'll hold them for you until then."

Virginia, stood on the street and watched as Mrs. McConnell robbed the mannequin of the coat and beret, placed them in a large white box and carried the box to the back of the store

"I'll have them paid for by Christmas," Virginia thought.

On Friday morning, Virginia heard Mr. Parks drop some mail in the mail box. She retrieved the mail and carried it inside. She fumbled through it as she walked down the hall to leave the mail on the mantle. She returned to her room clutching a letter from Bill as she walked down the hall. The letter was postmarked: Kershaw, South Carolina, October 6th, 1934 and read:

Kershaw, South Carolina
Sunday night

Dearest Pal,

I wonder what you are doing for yourself tonight. As for myself, I am watching the beautiful moon when I can see it. It is such a wonderful and beautiful night. I can hardly bear being here. It makes me think of you so much.

Virginia, I feel so bad tonight. I have a bad cold and these blues don't help any. I will be all right in a couple of days I guess. I'll let you know if it gets any worse. Hope you are not worrying or sick with your asthma again. I don't know if I will go to Gastonia one night this week or not. If I do, I will stop and get you or stay with you if you don't want to go anywhere. I will let you know about it later if the night does not slip upon me.

Well, its getting kind of late. I guess I had better go to bed and sleep a while if I can; if I can't I'll get up and watch the moon go down. I saw it set last night as I was coming home. It sure was beautiful. I got here okay. It was about ten until six. I stopped in Rock Hill to get a bit of grub. I have not finished my rum. I think I'll drink the rest before I go to bed. It makes me feel better. I don't make it a habit though.

I'm looking for a long sweet letter on Wednesday. I think so much of you Gin. So be good and true to me.

Only your,
Bill

P. S.

Please excuse this paper and writing as it is the best I can do tonight.

Saturday afternoon Virginia, Catherine, Isabelle, and Mary Lee walked downtown to the local movie to see *The Ghost and Mrs. Muir.* After the movie, they stopped by The Clover Drug to read the latest fashion magazines. Several other girls and boys mingled around the magazine rack making small talk.

"Did you hear about the Dalton brothers?" a young blonde headed boy asked.

"Oh, that's old news," Isabelle replied. "That happened weeks ago."

"I hear there're in Morganton with an aunt now," someone chimed in.

"Lucky there're not in jail," Mary Lee added.

"Maybe they'll stay out of trouble in Morganton," Isabelle commented.

"Not a chance," one of the boys added.

Virginia thumbed through the latest hairstyle magazine and was oblivious when Catherine slipped away to the front of the store. Later, she noticed her chatting with the same young man she had seen her with in front of Mr. Oren's store.

"Who's that handsome man I saw you talking with?" Virginia teased Catherine on the way home.

"Oh, nobody," Catherine replied. "Just someone I ran into in the drugstore one afternoon.

Virginia wanted to delve into the subject deeper but decided not to press her sister any further.

The hearty laughter of Virginia and Catherine's Aunt Erline echoed down the hall as they entered the house. They saw their Aunt Erline and Uncle Erwin in the sitting room. Uncle Ervin sat backward in a straight chair, as was his custom, intent in a discussion of his favorite topic, politics. Aunt Erline, listened intently, her hair shining like a copper penny in the window light. Red heads are quick tempered, Virginia had always heard, but not Aunt Erline. Aunt Erline was slow to anger as Virginia learned the day she broke her aunt's favorite tea pitcher. Virginia and Catherine both enjoyed Aunt Erline's bubbly sense of humor and Uncle Erwin's gentle nature.

Virginia and Catherine plopped down on the blue sofa underneath the picture of President Franklin Roosevelt.

"If mother would take that picture down," Virginia thought, "Uncle Erwin might forget about politics for a while."

Virginia and Catherine watched and listened as their mother and Aunt Erline rocked and talked, the rockers slowly traveling across the slick linoleum floor.

The conversation soon turned to the textile workers'strike or the *Strike of '29* as her father referred to it.

On April 1, 1929, workers at the Loray Mill in Gastonia, North Carolina walked off the job in protest of diminishing wages and deteriorating work conditions in the mill. The mill workers formed the National Textile Workers Union and demanded recognition of it. Tensions mounted and resulted in the death of Gastonia policeman, Chief Orville Atterholt and later Ella Louise Wiggins, one of the strike workers. Conditions in the mills did improve as a result but the mill workers very seldom ever spoke of the strike.

Virginia could not remember a time in her life that either one or both of her parents did not work in a textile mill. She herself had never even toured a textile mill. Instead, her parents had made a decision not to allow her in a mill because it might compromise her already delicate health. This only served to heighten her interest in the plight of the southern textile workers. Most of what Virginia knew about the *Strike of '29* she had gleaned from *The Clover Herald*, the local newspaper. She and Catherine remained silent on the sofa and soaked up the ensuing conversation.

Chapter 6

A subtle hint of the cold winter to follow arrived with the clear crisp air of October. When Virginia awoke each morning, fire danced in almost every fireplace to frighten away the chill of early morning. The brisk air on her walks to and from work refreshed her as she hugged her sweater tighter around her body. Golden leaves waved farewell to summer and floated to the ground to land at Virginia's feet. The store windows displayed the orange, brown, and red hues of Fall as Virginia passed and a fat, orange Jack-o-lantern smiled at her from Mr. Oren's window each morning as she arrived for work.

The morning hours passed swiftly for Virginia as she saw to the demands of Mr. Oren's customers on this Thursday morning. Shortly after noon, Catherine dropped in for a chat as she often did. She smiled at Virginia as she greeted her and at the same time reached inside her handbag.

"Thought you might want this," she said as she held the letter out to Virginia. "Mr. Parks left this for you this morning."

Virginia's face brightened as she reached for the letter.

"Thanks, Catherine," she replied.

Several customers entered the store and under the watchful eye of Mr. Oren, Virginia quickly stuffed the letter in her pocket. Catherine lingered in the store until a friend appeared and they soon left together to walk further up the street. Virginia said her goodbyes and watched as Catherine and her friend crossed the street. For a brief moment, Virginia longed to join them.

Unlike the morning, the afternoon crept by like the slow drip, drip of a faucet. Her eagerness to read Bill's letter only added to the dragging time. Virginia's asthma returned with the changing of the season and plagued her more frequently. Today was no exception and she found relief when Mr. Oren closed the store promptly at five o'clock.

Virginia approached a few friends on her way home and they tried to talk her into joining them at the diner but Virginia's thoughts were focused only on the letter in her pocket.

"I'm needed at home this afternoon, she replied to their pleadings. I'll join you another day."

Virginia's friends were far out of sight before she reached into her pocket and pulled the letter out. She scanned the postmark that read: Kershaw, South Carolina, Oct. 22, 1934. She opened the letter and the October wind tugged at the edge of the paper as her eyes traveled the familiar path through Bill's bold handwriting.

Kershaw, South Carolina
Monday, AM.

Dearest Pal,

I will write a few lines as I wait for a letter from you. I can hardly wait to get it. I was terribly blue both Saturday and Sunday, Gin. I have been at work since I left on Sunday. I worked hard for about eight hours yesterday. The rest of the time I've been making twelve hours a day. I am still at the mill.

I hear the train blowing now. Maybe I will get a letter on it. I hope so anyway. It does a lot of good to hear from you. I had one hundred times rather see you though. I will be working at night this week. Maybe I will get to see you because I am off both Saturday and Saturday night. I guess. I will let you know later when I write again. Guess I had better go see about the mail. Be back in a few minutes.

Well, nothing doing. I wonder if you got my letter on Saturday. I am still hoping, maybe, I'll get one from you this afternoon.

Gin, I hope you are better and that your asthma is not hindering you again. I hope you are not as blue as I am. I watched the moon part of Saturday and Sunday night. It sure was beautiful but it made me lonesome. It can't be long now before I see you again.

I guess I will quit off and sleep a while, if I can, because I have twelve hours to build tonight. I'll write more when I get your letter.

Tuesday, 2 o'clock

I just received your letter, Gin. I am sure glad to hear that you are some better. I was expecting a letter yesterday but got left.

No, I am not watching the moon with someone else. Maybe, you are watching the moon with some other guy. Is that why you mention it? I wouldn't think so.

Gin, I am waiting here at the post office trying to get this letter off on the 2 o'clock train. That is the reason I am writing on the back of what I had left yesterday. Please excuse it if you can get it straight.

Always your,
Bill

Virginia reread the letter several times and when she arrived home, she placed it in the cedar box with the others.

Nine days later, under a full harvest moon, Bill rode the train to Clover. Virginia met him at the depot and they walked hand in hand along the moonlit street. The fire in the fireplace at Virginia's home cast a warm glow on their faces as they sat together on the sofa. The clock in the hall too quickly chimed away the hours and over in the wee hours of the morning, Bill walked the moonlit street alone to Daniel's.

Bill returned in Daniel's car for Virginia by noon on Saturday morning. They enjoyed a quick lunch with Daniel and Anna Jane and then drove to Gastonia to visit Bill's cousin, Richard, and his wife, Molly. They stopped to see Gloria Swanson in *Music in the Air*, at the Webb Theatre and returned the car to Daniel just in time for him to take his family to the annual Halloween party at the church. Bill and Virginia tagged along and enjoyed the rambunctious children. After the party, Daniel dropped Bill and Virginia off at Virginia's home and they spent the remainder of their time together in the soft glow of the fire.

On Sunday morning, Bill and Virginia attended church services at the Methodist Church and after a quick lunch at the diner, Bill caught the train to Kershaw. He waved goodbye to Virginia from the window as the train pulled away and Virginia found it difficult to smile. When she turned to walk away, the sound of the train whistle pierced the air.

"How quickly time flies when Bill is here," she thought as she walked alone down the sidewalk. "It's only a few weeks until Thanksgiving. Maybe, he'll be back then."

The even lower temperatures of November prompted Virginia's father to drive her to work each day. She missed the short walks to work and the time alone it offered her. Asthma continued to disrupt her life from time to time but robbed her of only one day at Mr. Oren's. On the days when her health did confine her to bed, she spent the time writing letters to Bill. Her mother and father had softened their opinion of Bill and on occasion, inquired about his welfare. The lower temperatures of November necessitated that all fireplaces be kept in constant use and this alone kept Catherine and Virginia busy as it fell to them to keep them burning. Virginia hated to carry the clunky pieces of wood that often left splinters in her arms.

Business at Mr. Oren's dime store improved because of the approaching holiday season. Even though times were hard, the inexpensive items in Mr. Oren's store were within reach for most and Virginia's days flew by as the store filled more and more with Mr. Oren's customers.

On a Friday night in late November, Virginia heard a knock on the door.

"I hope it's Bill," she thought and rushed to answer the door.

Her hopes were dashed, however, when she opened the door and there stood the handsome young man she had seen talking to Catherine.

"Hello, I'm Thomas McCall. Is Catherine here?" he asked glancing down at the floor.

"Come on in," Virginia replied. "I'll get her for you."

Virginia ushered the young man into the living room and he took a seat on the sofa in front of the fire. Catherine soon joined him there.

"Why didn't you tell me about him?" Virginia teased, when Catherine's guest departed.

"I don't know," Catherine replied. "I guess I just wanted to keep him a secret for a while"

"Too late," Virginia continued to tease. "The cat's out of the bag now."

Catherine blushed as Virginia continued and although she was happy for her sister, Virginia inwardly wished that the knock on the door had been Bill's.

Thomas called on Catherine every weekend and on these occasions Virginia missed her sister's company.

Chapter 7

The landscape of November showcased the stark dreariness of winter. Virginia could hardly remember the brilliant hues of Fall. The fireplaces weren't enough now to scare the chill away and most mornings when Virginia arose, the house felt drafty and cold. The first thing upon rising, Virginia chunked more wood on the fire to warm the room well by the time she dressed for work. Mr. Oren's store bustled with customers and Virginia welcomed the business. Time seemed to fly and Thanksgiving was in sight, only a short time away. Catherine and Virginia had managed to talk their parents into an invitation for both Bill and Thomas for Thanksgiving dinner. It was Virginia's hope that once they knew Bill better, they might find him as charming as they found Thomas. Thomas was a ruggedly handsome man who possessed a quiet nature and easy manner. His kind nature seldom offended and he was as comfortable as a warm blanket on a winter day. After high school, wanderlust lured Thomas to the grain fields out West. He had recently returned to Clover and found gainful employment at Southern Electric Power, the local power company. Thomas received much favor from Virginia's parents.

Bill's job in Kershaw kept him in the mill twelve hours a day all week and most weekends. His letters to Virginia suffered due to the long hours. In his last letter to her, he spoke of his pleasure in the Thanksgiving dinner invitation.

"Are you certain your family won't mind?" Bill inquired in his last letter, aware of the cool reception he might possibly experience. "I know your family well enough already," he teasingly wrote. "But I do look forward to meeting Thomas. I'll write again before Thanksgiving and let you know when I'll be in."

On Saturday night, Thomas came by to call on Catherine and they went to Gastonia. They urged Virginia to go with them but not desiring to be a tag-a-long, she declined choosing instead to remain behind and help her mother with a grocery list for the Thanksgiving meal, now only two weeks away.

The following afternoon Virginia arrived from work to find a letter on her dresser from Bill. She glanced at the postmark that read: Kershaw, South Carolina, November 14, 1934 and eagerly opened the letter to read the hastily scribbled message.

Kershaw, South Carolina
Monday, AM

Dearest Virginia,

Not much time to write today and I want to get this off to you on the next train out. I will be in Clover on Wednesday the 23rd. Please meet me at the depot at six o'clock. I'll be leaving again on Sunday but we will have a few days together. Dropped Daniel a line and I will be staying there for that weekend. Well, got to go. I hear the train about to leave.

Forever your,
Bill

Virginia folded the letter and went over to the cedar box on her dresser. She removed the letters from the box, untied the blue ribbon that held them together, and placed the letter on top.

"Mother," she shouted from the hallway. "Bill will be here for Thanksgiving."

"Guess you're pretty happy about that," her mother replied.

"I am," Virginia said entering the room where her mother stood ironing. "When you get to know him, you'll change your mind about him."

"We'll see," her mother replied with a sigh. "We'll see."

The week of Thanksgiving, Virginia and Catherine spent every available moment in preparation for the holiday meal. Catherine made numerous trips to the local grocer while Virginia cleaned, polished, and waxed every piece of furniture until they sparkled like newly fallen dew. On Wednesday, Virginia, Catherine, and their mother spent the entire day in the kitchen. The wonderful aromas of the special holiday foods filled the house and Virginia' excitement mounted each time the clock chimed away another hour.

Later in the afternoon, Bertha knocked on the door and Virginia's mother invited her in. A basket of food, still warm from the stove, sat by the door and held enough food for Bertha and her family.

When she noticed the bulging basket, she smiled and said, "Sure do thank you Miss Nivens. Sure do. My children look forward to this every year."

"You're welcome," Virginia's mother answered. "It's no trouble at all. "There's more than enough here for everyone."

Bertha hung around to help clean the kitchen and place one of her pristine white tablecloths on the table.

The afternoon slipped by and at five o'clock, Virginia left the kitchen to prepare herself for Bill's arrival. She donned a winter white sweater and a brown wool skirt to keep her warm at the depot. She gathered her hair back with a brown satin ribbon. Around her neck she wore the delicate wooden cross on the gold chain. When Virginia took her brown coat from the coat rack, she thought of the bright red coat that would hang in its place by Christmas and smiled.

At five forty- five Virginia's father drove her to the depot. The train arrived promptly on time at six and Virginia watched expectantly as each passenger departed, the wind whipping around her ankles as she stood waiting for Bill. When the last passenger departed, Virginia couldn't quench the sinking sensation she felt. Bill had not arrived on the train and Virginia was overwhelmed with disappointment.

"But he said he would be here," she thought. "How could he do this?" "He knew how much I was looking forward to this."

Virginia remained silent on the ride home.

"Everything will be okay, Virginia," her father said to console her.

"I can't imagine what happened to him," Virginia replied.

When they arrived home, Virginia went straight to her room, leaving her father to break the news to her mother. She couldn't bear to hear the critical words she knew awaited. Virginia turned on the radio and tried to soothe her unhappiness with music.

"Virginia," she heard her mother call.

Virginia turned the volume down on the radio when she heard her mother say,

"Virginia, you have a visitor."

Virginia rose from the bed, did a hasty repair on her hair, and stepped out into the hallway. There in the dim light stood Bill.

"Sorry I'm late," he apologized. "I caught a ride with a fellow at work who lives in York. Hope you're not upset. I thought we would beat the train but I was wrong."

At that moment, nothing mattered to Virginia except that Bill had arrived for Thanksgiving.

Thanksgiving Day revealed itself clear, cold, and crisp. The fire in the fireplaces popped and crackled as they consumed the fresh chunks of wood. The aroma of the holiday meal permeated each room of the house and the dining room table beckoned with its attractive array of mismatched dishes.

Thomas and Bill arrived within fifteen minutes of each other and Virginia and Catherine left them together in the cozy front room to catch up on things while they helped in the kitchen. Soon, they heard the familiar laughter of Uncle Ervin and Aunt Erline as they arrived with their two children, Daisy and James. Everyone gathered around the table and the room filled with lively chatter and laughter.

A cold November rain fell throughout the weekend. Daniel loaned Bill his car on Saturday and he and Virginia rode to Gastonia. The swish of the windshield wipers and the all encompassing rain cocooned them in the car as the dreary landscape passed serenely by. When they arrived in Gastonia, Bill parked the car in front of Woolworth's Department Store. They darted into the store for a light meal at the lunch counter and they spent some time later browsing through the stores on Main Street. Around three o'clock, they ducked into the Webb Theater for a matinee. Even the noise of the movie did not drown out the sound of the rain or the occasional loud clap of thunder that jarred everyone in their seats. The sky hung heavy with rain as they left the theatre and Virginia waited under the awning of the theatre until Bill brought the car around. The florescent light of the marquee reflected like Christmas lights onto the side of the wet car as Bill pulled up in front of the theatre. The colorful lights complimented Virginia as she stood in their reflection and did not go unnoticed by Bill.

The rain glistened in the car lights, collected in the low places in the road, and splashed upon the car as they passed. Bill remained silent, deep in thought, as they traveled along.

"Bill, is anything wrong?" Virginia asked. "You're terribly quiet.

"Virginia", Bill answered, "I'm hoping that before long I'll find a steady job with better pay. The kind of job a man with a wife needs. When I do, will you marry me? I know I don't have much to offer right now but... "

"Bill, I'll marry you," Virginia interrupted him to say. "I'll marry you," and reached for his hand.

On Sunday afternoon, Bill returned to Kershaw on the train. As Virginia waved goodbye the usual melancholy that accompanied his departure escaped her. Their plans for the future had driven it away.

The cold, wet weather hastened an onset of asthma for Virginia and she spent the next couple of days confined to bed.

She missed a day of work at the dime store but Mr. Oren lived up to his word and was tolerant of the situation. On Thursday, she returned to work in time to decorate the front window for Christmas. As Virginia placed the ornaments on the tree, she smiled and thought of the red coat. After only two more payments the coat would belong to her. For weeks she had saved money to buy presents for her family and smiled at thought of Christmas only a few weeks away. The mill had stood two days out of every week for the last few months creating a financial hardship on the family. Catherine found work in the local beauty salon and Virginia was proud that she and Catherine's wages provided some relief. Virginia realized that with the country, not yet free from the grip of the depression, Christmas would prove hard for most this year. Virginia had received one letter from Bill since Thanksgiving and in it he spoke again of the long hours and low wages in the mill. There was nothing to be done but endure as jobs were scarce and any job at all was better than none. At least for a while, Bill had steady work when others were not so fortunate. Virginia knew that it could not last forever.

Chapter 8

Virginia's father arrived at Mr. Oren's store promptly at five o'clock on a December Thursday and pulled into an empty parking space in front of the store. Virginia tied her brown wool scarf tightly around her neck and hurried to the car.

"This came for you today," her father said as she slipped into the seat beside him. "How was your day?" he inquired holding the letter out to her.

"Thank you," Virginia said as she took the letter from his hand. "Everything was fine today. We're busier than ever now that Christmas is so close."

"Can't believe it's almost Christmas," her father replied.

Virginia slid the letter into the pocket of her brown wool coat as she hung the coat on the coat rack.

"I'll save this for later." She thought.

Catherine arrived home shortly after Virginia and they both went to the kitchen to help their mother. Most of the conversation around the dinner table centered on the arrival of Christmas and all it would entail. Virginia and Catherine decided on a day to shop for presents and promised to help with Christmas preparations.

After dinner, Virginia paused long enough in the hall to retrieve the letter from Bill from her coat pocket. She saw Kershaw, South Carolina, December 19, 8:30 a.m., 1934 stamped on the front of the envelope. She continued to her room, shut the door, and slid the letter from its envelope.

Kershaw S.C.
Tuesday night

Hello Dearest,

I received your letter after so long a time but I sure was glad to hear from you. Just think, from Wednesday until Tuesday, of course I don't know how my letters have been serving you although I did write if you didn't get them. You have been sick. That's it. You wouldn't let me know it. I need not talk though, for I've been sick too. I believe I have T. B. I've almost coughed myself to death for two weeks. I am a lot better now. Although I have been sick, I haven't missed but a couple of days work last week. I am working plenty this week, every day.

I hope you are a lot better. I don't like for my best pal to be like that. I don't suppose you can help it though. I can't.

Talking about when I will see you. If I had my way I would see you tonight because I want to be with you always. It looks as if I will have to wait for a while though. I don't know exactly what day I will be there, Virginia. I don't know how long we will get for Christmas. Don't care much because I am going to take what I want. Any ole way, I'll be with you some day. I may be there Sunday night and stay through Tuesday or Wednesday. I don't know so when you see me coming you can say I'll be there. I know that is poor satisfaction but it is the best I can do at the present. Maybe I can tell you better the last of next week. Just think about it. In a few short days I will be with my best pal. I was looking at that beautiful moon a little while ago and could hardly believe that it is almost Christmas. Speaking of the moon, I saw it for a few minutes and then beautiful white clouds covered it. It is now starting to sleet or rain or something. I think it's going to hail next. It has done every thing but that. I hope it will be pretty on Christmas. Of course I can enjoy it just as well with you in bad weather. I am happiest when I am with you, even if it's stormy. Come to think of it, I have been happy with you when it was stormy. Those are the good ole days.

Well, I am tired and sleepy so I will go to see you only in dreams. I am looking for a long letter from you.. I will answer so you will get it by Saturday. I hope. So long pal until we meet again.

Only your,
Bill

P.S. Meet me at the depot Christmas Eve at six o'clock. Sorry I can't come sooner but I will have a couple days to spend with you after Christmas.

Bill

The cold, clear weather of December heralded in the Christmas season. Catherine accompanied Virginia to McConnell's Department Store on a bitter cold December morning to give Mrs. McConnell the final payment on the red coat and pancake beret.

"You'll look lovely in these," Mrs. McConnell commented as she handed Virginia the box that had protected the coat and beret for the last few months.

"Thank you, Mrs. McConnell," Virginia replied as she opened the box. "There're even prettier than I remembered," Virginia said replacing the lid on the box.

Virginia and Catherine tarried in town long enough to watch Thomas as he helped string the multicolored Christmas lights from one side of Main Street to the other. Catherine blushed when Thomas noticed her from the top of a pole and winked. Everyone in Clover would gather in town on Friday for the annual Christmas parade and afterward the lights would officially welcome in the holiday season. Already, holiday cheer abounded in the smiles and greetings of Mr. Oren's customers.

"This will be a wonderful Christmas," Virginia commented to Catherine as they stood on the street and watched the workers.

"I know," Catherine replied. "I think it will be the best ever." "Will Bill be here for Christmas?"

"I hope he'll be here by Christmas Eve," Virginia answered.

The remainder of the day, Virginia and Catherine shopped the stores for Christmas gifts. When they arrived home, they eagerly decorated the cedar tree their father had brought home the previous night. Virginia, Catherine, and their mother gathered at the foot of the tree to wrap gifts. The scent of the cedar tree filled the room and the fire reflected onto the contented countenance of Virginia's face.

December 24th appeared clear and icy cold. The house bustled with the preparations for Christmas dinner. Virginia and Catherine helped the entire morning in the kitchen and then began a series of household chores. Thomas had accepted the invitation for Christmas dinner and Catherine hummed as she helped her mother. Virginia thought about nothing else but Bill and the time they would have together. The atmosphere in the room was electric with excitement and expectation.

"Virginia, do you need me to take you to the depot this afternoon?" her father asked. "There's talk of snow and it's pretty cold out there."

"No thanks, Daddy. I'll walk. I'll be warm in my new beret and coat."

"Alright then," her father answered. "But if you change your mind let me know."

Late in the afternoon, Virginia donned a black wool sweater and black skirt. She combed her dark hair to softly frame her face and added just a touch of red lipstick to her lips. She slipped the red coat over her sweater and skirt and pinned the matching beret in her hair. Her reflection in the mirror pleased her.

The air carried an unusual chill as Virginia walked toward the depot and she quickened her steps. To her relief, the train arrived right on time and she eagerly searched the crowd for Bill. The red coat and beret caught Bill's attention immediately as he stepped from the train loosing no time in approaching her.

"You look beautiful Virginia," he commented as they embraced. "It's so good to see you"

"Thank you," Virginia answered as his hand found hers. A light snow began to fall as they walked the sidewalk toward her home.

"Just what we wanted," Bill said.

"Yes it is," Virginia answered. "This will be the best Christmas ever."

By morning, everything in sight was wrapped in the white splendor of snow. Thomas plowed through it all in his car and arrived early for Christmas dinner. Daniel dropped Bill off shortly before noon and Bill and Thomas enjoyed each other's company in front of the fire while last minute preparations were completed on the meal. The aroma of holiday food and the scent of the cedar Christmas tree created a festive holiday mood as the fire crackled in the fireplace.

Around the dinner table there was much discussion about the country and how the depression had impacted almost every avenue of employment.

"How is the mill running in Kershaw?" Virginia's father inquired of Bill.

"Right now things are okay but it can't last much longer. I'd say that in about a month the mill could come to a standstill," Bill answered

"Rough time of year for that," Virginia's father replied. "I think the Hawthorne and the Thread might stand two days a week for a while but rumor is they'll pick back up to five days before too much longer. Maybe we'll start to see the country pull out of the depression soon."

"A lot of people will see a rough winter," Thomas added. "Some of our best customers are already finding it difficult to pay their power bill. Roosevelt is doing what he can but it'll just take some time."

The conversation continued for quite some time before Virginia's mother suggested that the men retire to the living room while the women cleaned the kitchen.

Virginia and Catherine helped their mother in the kitchen until every dish was washed and stacked neatly in the cupboard. Afterward, they carried cups of hot coffee to the living room along with a tray of Christmas cookies. Outside, snow began to fall as they sat by the fire in quiet conversation.

In mid afternoon, Thomas and Catherine decided to take a walk in the snow.

"Come go with us," Thomas said. "We won't be gone long."

"No thanks," Virginia replied. "It's much too cold for me."

"Me too," Bill added. "We'll wait for you right here in front of the fire."

Virginia and Bill watched Catherine and Thomas from the window as they walked hand in hand through the snow. Their voices echoed from far down the street before Virginia and Bill settled back on the sofa in front of the fire. Warmed by the fire, the boughs on the mantle filled the room with the fresh scent of pine. Bill and Virginia sat, content in the silence, watching the fire until Bill rose from the sofa and lifted a brightly wrapped box from under the pine boughs on the mantle. He turned and walked over to Virginia.

"Merry Christmas and Happy Birthday," Bill said as he placed a small package in Virginia's hand.

Chapter 9

Two days later Bill caught the train for Kershaw.

"I'll be back soon," he said as he boarded the train.

"I'll be waiting," Virginia replied.

Virginia watched the train depart and began the lonesome walk home. Piles of dirty snow lay along the side of the road and mirrored her mood. Thoughts of Christmas consumed her mind as she walked along and she glanced at the gold heart dangling from the charm bracelet on her wrist, Bill's Christmas gift to her. She held the heart steady in her hand and read the word, *Forever,* on the front then turned it over to read the inscription, *Your Bill,* on the back. The excitement of Christmas had departed on the same train that carried Bill back to Kershaw and left Virginia melancholy in its absence.

Soon, a car pulled up beside her and a voice called out,

"Hop in." We're on our way to the movie. Wanna go?"

Virginia glanced over and saw Thomas and Catherine.

She opened the car door and slid into the back seat.

"We've been looking for you," Catherine said. "Want to go to the movie with us." "*Forsaking All Others* is playing at the Sylvia in York and I know you like Clark Gable."

"Okay," Virginia replied and welcomed any distraction from her present mood.

A tiny glimmer of light reflected from the engagement ring on her sister's left hand, Thomas' Christmas gift to Catherine.

On Tuesday morning, Virginia returned to work. The town appeared void of life after the bustle of Christmas. Stripped of its colorful holiday attire, it now matched the dreary landscape of winter. Virginia noticed Thomas high on a telephone pole and called to him. He smiled and waved in return. Strings of colorful lights lay coiled at the bottom of the telephone poles awaiting their return to the large boxes lined at intervals along the street.

Virginia spent most of her day removing the last vestiges of Christmas from the store. A few customers wandered in and out and Virginia joined in idle conversation with them. She enjoyed the lively renditions of their Christmas experiences. The Dalton brothers had returned home for Christmas and with the frequent admonishments from their parents, they managed to give the town a reprieve from their usual antics. The talk was that they might be home for good in the Spring.

Anna Jane, followed by her three children, stopped in for some friendly conversation. The children beamed as they held up new toys for Virginia to see.

"Looks as if Santa stopped by your house after all," Virginia teased the children.

"How was your Christmas?" Anna Jane inquired.

"It was a wonderful Christmas with Bill and Thomas to share it with us," Virginia replied. "The time flew by much too fast though. It seems as if Bill just got here before I found myself at the depot waving goodbye. Thomas surprised Catherine with an engagement ring and they are considering a wedding in early spring. We all think a lot of Thomas and Catherine floats on air these days."

"Sounds as if it was an extremely good Christmas," Anna Jane replied. "The wedding will give us something to look forward to. Do you think they'll marry in the church?"

"Oh, yes," Virginia replied. "If mother has anything at all to do with it they will, even though Thomas comes from a large family and they alone will fill up our small church."

Anna Jane and the children remained in the store for a few more minutes and then headed toward the grocery store.

"Come by to see us," she called back to Virginia before she left the store. "We'd love to have you over for supper."

"I'll see you soon," Virginia replied. "Bill and I might drop by when he comes home. I know he'd enjoy one of your home cooked meals."

"We look forward to seeing you then," Anna Jane replied. "We'll, see you later then."

"Okay," Virginia replied as Anna Jane and the children disappeared through the door.

The advent of 1935 carried with it both optimism and trepidation for Virginia. The aftermath of the depression still held a steady grip on the country and refused to let go. Instead, it promised greater hardship in the coming year. But Virginia continued to fan a tiny flame of optimism as if by sheer will, she might capture the elusive reforms the country so needed.

Friday night, at the stroke of midnight, the New Year marched in to the slow steady cadence of struggle and Virginia joined in the march.

A few days later, Virginia received a much awaited letter from Bill. The postmark read: Kershaw, South Carolina, January 5th, 11a.m. Virginia opened the envelope and began to read a hastily scribbled note from Bill.

Kershaw, S.C.
Wednesday morning

Dearest Pal,

Sorry I couldn't write sooner. Sure is a let down after Christmas to find myself here in Kershaw again. When I went to work Monday morning the rumor was that there is only about two more weeks of work left here. I knew it couldn't last much longer but I counted on being here a little longer. Daniel mentioned at Christmas that there might be an opening at the Hawthorne fairly soon. I'll drop a line to him and see if he can help me out. It would be a lucky break to start the New Year out with you. I could get a room at the boarding house. What do you think? Hope you're not as blue and lonesome as I am. I'll close for now and try to get this on the train before my break is over. Write soon.

Forever your,
Bill

Bill returned to Clover the fourth week in January. With Daniel's help, he secured a job in the Hawthorne from eight a.m. until four p.m. and moved in with Daniel until a room became available in the boarding house. Virginia saw his return as a good omen that 1935 would hold better days for them. The long distance relationship had been difficult at best and Bill's return came at just the right time.

As if an ally to the depression, the winter held a tight grip on the country with its frigid temperatures and added to its plight. But after a heavy snowfall in March, winter breathed its final sigh and relented to the warm caress of spring.

Thomas and Catherine were married on a fresh spring afternoon at St. Peter's Methodist Church, the quaint country church of Catherine's youth. Her bouquet of jonquils and lily of the valley gave visible evidence of their hope for new beginnings. They settled into a modest frame home closer to town that Thomas paid cash for. Catherine, for the first time in her young life, lived in a home that wasn't owned by the mill.

Part 11
Marriage

Chapter 10

The summer of 1935, as if an offspring of the previous summer, mimicked its sweltering temperatures and high humidity. Virginia held tight to her job at Mr. Oren's and squirreled away as much of her income as possible. She and Bill spent every free moment together and the summer escaped as a misty vapor.

On a hot day in late June, Bertha ambled up the walk. Virginia's mother greeted her from the rocker on the porch with "Good morning, Bertha. I'm glad you're here early this morning. Looks like today's gonna be a hot one and the cool of the morning is libel to be all the relief we get. The clothes are already in the back yard."

"Yes ma'am," Bertha answered and continued on around the house to the back yard.

A fire crackled under the black iron wash pot as Bertha dropped the clothes in and stirred them in the boiling water. Beads of sweat already glistened on her forehead and she stopped long enough to tie a red cloth around her head.

"Sure enough quiet around her since Miss Catherine married," Bertha said as she hung wet clothes on the line. "It's sure enough quiet."

"I know," Virginia's mother answered. "She comes to visit most every Sunday afternoon though. Thank goodness I still have Virginia to keep me good company what time she's not with Bill."

"Better keep an eye on that Bill," Bertha replied. "Else you'll be losing Virginia next."

"Bill does have steady work now but there's still something about him that puts me off. Maybe it's just his shy ways," Mrs. Nivens continued.

"Aw, Bill's okay," Bertha answered. "He's just awfully quiet. It makes you wonder what he's thinking. Miss Virginia's sure is fond of him. That's plain."

"That's plain alright," Mrs. Nivens added. "I just hope she's not making a mistake putting all her eggs in that basket."

"You can't do anything about it. No ma'am, you can't do anything about it," Bertha answered. "Miss Virginia's mind is made up. It's sure enough made up."

The oppressive temperature of the bedroom woke Virginia from her sleep and forced her from the bedroom to the kitchen for a drink of ice water. The voices from the yard captured her attention and she peeped out the kitchen window.

"Oh, no," she moaned when she spotted Bertha and her mother toiling over the clothes. "It's wash day."

Virginia sat in the kitchen for a few minutes and then called from the open window, "Need some help?"

"Come help Bertha hang these clothes," her mother answered.

The three of them worked on the clothes until midday and after a light lunch, Bertha ambled down the walkway in pursuit of her next job.

That night, Bill picked Virginia up in Daniel's car and they joined Daniel and Anna Jane for an evening meal. They arrived early and Virginia went to the kitchen to help Anna Jane while Daniel and Bill remained in the living room in a deep discussion about the economy.

Daniel turned to Bill during a lull in the conversation and said, "Bill, I know where there's a house that'll be up for rent soon. A fellow in my department at work is moving his family to York in a few weeks. "The house will be empty," Daniel continued. "It's over on Smith Street and within walking distance of work. It's just the right size for you. Why don't you inquire about it and get out of the boarding house? You'll have more privacy and room."

"Exactly where is Smith Street?" Bill inquired.

"Get Virginia to show you when you take her home. I know she knows where it is," Daniel answered.

"I'll check into that," Bill answered. "Might be just the thing I need."

Anna Jane called to Daniel and Bill from the kitchen to join them there. An energetic conversation ensued and time escaped them without notice. Later, Anna Jane glanced at the clock on the kitchen wall and shooed the children off to bed. She and Virginia cleared the table of dishes and Daniel retrieved a deck of cards from the desk drawer. He shuffled the cards and a lively game began. As hard as Daniel tried he could never beat Bill at cards and was reluctant to forfeit the effort until the hour grew late. Daniel finally gave in and Bill teased him as he rose to take Virginia home.

"Better luck next time," he chided as he and Virginia went out the door.

"Yea," Daniel answered and shut the door.

The hands of the clock in the square read eleven forty-five when Bill and Virginia rode through town. The silence in the car conveyed to Virginia that Bill's thoughts had wandered somewhere else. A light mist covered the windshield and the swish of the windshield wipers only magnified the silence.

"Virginia," Bill's voice broke the silence. "Don't you think we should make some plans of our own?"

"What do you mean Bill?" Virginia asked.

I'm making reasonable money now and Daniel knows of a home on Smith Street that will be vacant soon. Do you know where Smith Street is?"

"Yes, and I think I know the house Daniel is talking about. It's not far. Turn left on Smith Street and I'll point it out to you." Virginia replied.

As soon as Bill turned onto Smith Street, they rounded a curb and Virginia pointed to a small, white frame house.

"Looks sort of small," Bill said when he spotted the house. "It's big enough though. I'm making fair money and could probably cover the rent on it." Bill paused for a minute and then continued, "Virginia, let's get married. With what I make and what you make at Mr. Oren's we should be okay. What do you think?"

A week passed before Virginia summoned the courage to tell her parents of the plans she and Bill had discussed. Her mother was cool about Bill's proposal for two days before she finally warmed up to the idea of the marriage. She had hoped that Virginia might stay at home a while longer. After all, she had hardly had time to adjust to the absence of Catherine since her marriage. Nevertheless, she realized that in a few short weeks she would find her nest empty.

On a bright Sunday in June, Bill and Virginia followed in Thomas and Catherine's footsteps and married at St. Peter's Methodist Church, the same church where they first met. Virginia said her marriage vows in a white suit and matching hat, as the sweet scent of the white roses and lilies of the valley filled the small sanctuary. Bill and Virginia spent their first night of marriage in the small frame house on Smith Street.

The days flew by while Bill and Virginia worked feverishly to paint and furnish their new home. The Hawthorne Mill continued to keep its employees in steady work and with the added income from Virginia's job at Mr. Oren's, Bill and Virginia began to plan for the future. Virginia's asthma improved and gave her a respite during the early weeks of her marriage.

Daniel and Anna Jane visited often and the two couples spent most evenings on the porch in conversation as the children chased fireflies on the lawn. Thomas and Catherine came by for visits and quite frequently they all went to the movies. The summer proved easy as warm breezes carried it onward into fall.

A jack-o-lantern smiled from the porch at Halloween as Virginia greeted trick-or-treaters with home baked cookies. She burned the turkey at Thanksgiving but a last minute invitation to her parents for dinner saved the holiday. Their modest home filled at Christmas with family and friends and laughter enveloped every room of their first home together. The seasons of 1935 were as fleeting as summer showers.

By August of 1935, the aftermath of the Depression loosened its grip in some parts of the country but textiles in the South continued to hold on by a thread. Rumors of layoffs began to swirl around the mill but Bill chose not to give much attention to them.

"No need to borrow trouble," he thought.

Late one August afternoon, Daniel knocked on Bill and Virginia's door. Bill came to the door a little surprised to see Daniel standing there.

"Let's take a ride," Daniel said. "We won't be gone long."

"Okay," Bill answered. "Let me tell Virginia first."

Daniel barely spoke as they rode through town.

"Is something on your mind Daniel?" Bill inquired.

"Yea," Daniel answered. "I'm afraid there's going to be some layoffs at the mill. Don't know how soon or how many but there will be some layoffs. Bill, I think you need to start looking for something else pretty quick because you'll probably be one of the first to go since you were one of the last hired.

"I sure hate to hear that," Bill answered. It might mean that I'll have to leave town to find work and Virginia won't take to that us just starting out and all."

"I thought I might let you know now so that when it comes you'll be ahead of the game," Daniel continued.

"I appreciate that," Bill answered.

The ride home gave Bill enough time to decide not to tell Virginia just yet. Instead he kept it to himself and began to inquire around about available work in other towns in case the layoff did come. The thought of it kept him up most nights.

Two weeks later, Bill came home with the bad news. Virginia didn't take the news well and by the time Bill explained to her that he would be forced to take a job in Newberry, South Carolina, she was in tears.

"I can't believe this is happening to us, Bill" Virginia sobbed.

"I want you to move back in with your parents for a while," Bill said. "I can't leave you here in this house alone when I'm gone."

"Oh, no, Bill," Virginia sobbed. "We've worked so hard to get the house the way we want it. I don't want to leave it now."

"Virginia, you know your health isn't that good and I can't leave you here alone," Bill replied.

"But Bill," Virginia sobbed louder. "I can…."

"No, Virginia. It's final. You've got to move back with your parents. I'll send for you as soon as I get settled in Newberry. I'll find us another house. It won't take long."

"But Bill, I don't want to leave here. We just got the house the way we want it and we'll lose the money we put into it," Virginia sobbed.

"We don't have that much in it," Bill answered. "And I can't leave you here alone. We'll save what money we can for a down payment on a house of our own."

"That will take forever," Virginia continued.

"No it won't," Bill replied. "Maybe I could find a place in Newberry just as nice as this one."

"I hate this, Bill," Virginia whined.

'It's the only solution right now," he answered.

A week later, Bill moved Virginia back in with her parents. Virginia tried to avoid the, I- told -you- so, look in her mother's eyes. Instead she focused on the time she had left with Bill.

Two days later, she walked with Bill down the familiar street to the depot.

"I can't believe this is happening to us," Virginia said.

"I know," Bill replied. "But it won't be long before I send for you. Meanwhile, just keep busy and the time will fly. You'll see. You need to take good care of yourself so that you'll be in good health when I send for you."

Daniel and Anna Jane drove up beside them and Bill and Virginia crawled into the back seat of the car.

"If there is any change at the mill, I'll drop you a line, Bill," Daniel said as he pulled away from the curb. "Anna Jane and I will check on Virginia every other day. Everything will work out okay in time."

"Thanks Daniel," Bill replied. "I appreciate that."

The train whistle blew and Bill stood with bags in hand to board. He quickly hugged and kissed Virginia good-bye and disappeared inside the train.

Daniel, Anna Jane, and Virginia stared at the train until it escaped their sight before they returned to the car. No one spoke a word until they arrived at Virginia's parents' home.

"I'll check on you in a couple of days," Daniel said as Virginia exited the car.

"Thanks Daniel," Virginia answered.

"Tough break for them," Daniel said as he pulled from the curb.

"Things will be better soon," Anna Jane replied. "I hope."

Chapter 11

Virginia awoke from a restless sleep the following morning and reached across the bed for Bill. It took only seconds to realize that she was not in her home on Smith Street and that Bill was gone. She closed her eyes again and listened to the clatter made by her mother in the kitchen. The room where she lay remained unchanged in her absence as if awaiting her return. Who could have predicted that the carefree young girl who rushed out the door to marry Bill would return in so short a time, this mature young woman? She listened to the hall clock tick away the minutes and made new plans, plans she had no choice but to make.

Virginia immersed herself in work at Mr. Oren's, grateful for the diversion from the situation she now found herself in. She waited each day for a letter from Bill.

Two weeks passed before Virginia returned from work to discover a letter from Bill lying on her dresser. The postmark read: October 11th, 8 a.m., Newberry, South Carolina.

"At last," Virginia thought as she opened the letter and began to read.

Newberry, South Carolina
Thursday

Hello Darling,

I haven't received a letter from you but I am writing to you anyway. Hope you haven't lost the address I left with you. I guess I have a letter at the J.R.C. but I am so tired and it is about a mile over there. I am working now, honey, and moved my boarding place. It is only costing me $20.00 to stay here a month. I just moved over here night before last. I wish you were with me tonight. Maybe this time next Thursday night, you will. I haven't gotten straightened out yet. I don't know what to do. I'm glad I've got work but I don't know how long it will last. It might last until Christmas or longer, possibly even longer. But anyway, I am going to try to see by Sunday. If not, you will receive the money to come down here. I hate to be away from you like this but I can't help it. I could have seen you before now if I had known that I was not going to work before Monday but I didn't know that. I am working like h…, Gin. It is a pain but I think I can take it. I will tell you all about it when you come down here. I just may get somebody to bring me to see you if I can.

Gin, is your health any better? I have worried that your asthma has gotten worse. You are always on my mind.

Please write to me when you get this in case I don't get there to see you. Send it to the same address here because I do not know the address here and everybody has gone to the big circus in town. I have no one to ask. I am here all alone, darling.

Virginia, I hope you are not worrying yourself to death about me. Remember to be well when I call for you. It won't be many more days.

Yes, I notice the moon every night. It is very beautiful tonight. Wish you could be with me.

So long,
Your, Bill

Bill did not arrive on Sunday as he had hoped. But instead, on Wednesday, Virginia received a train ticket to Newberry in the mail from him. Along with the ticket, he included instructions to meet him at the depot, five o'clock, Friday afternoon.

The click-clack of the train eased some of Virginia's anxiousness as she gazed from the train window. A small boy and his mother sat in the seat in front of her and soon the young boy befriended her. She made easy conversation with his mother and learned that they were returning to Newberry from a week with her parents in York. Virginia quizzed her about Newberry and explained that she too was traveling to Newberry to meet her husband.

"You'll love Newberry," the boy's mother said. "We moved there about three years ago and find it an excellent place for family life. My husband works for the city."

"My husband moved to Newberry a few weeks ago," Virginia replied. "And this is my first trip to see him. I'm looking forward to the weekend. I should be joining him when he finds a suitable place for us."

"I hope you won't have much trouble.

"We'll find something soon," Virginia replied.

The train depot appeared in the distance and Virginia's anxiousness returned. She strained to look ahead.

The young boy, now asleep in his mother's lap, began to whine as she roused him from his sleep.

"Wake up, Billy," she said. "We're almost home."

The child rubbed his eyes and gazed out the train window. His mother gathered their luggage and handed a small brown suitcase to her son. He smiled and hugged it tightly to his chest. Virginia noticed the excitement in the young boy's expression.

"I'll see Dad soon. Won't I, Mom?" he asked.

"You certainly will," she answered.

She smiled at her son as he turned to gaze out the window.

"We're in Newberry," Virginia thought. "I hope Bill isn't late."

The train pulled into the depot and Virginia saw Bill standing on the platform. She gave a sigh of relief and waved from the window. He rushed to greet her as she stepped from the train and they walked hand in hand. Virginia saw the young boy and his mother as they greeted a handsome young man and Virginia sensed that he must be the young boy's father. She waved a quick good-bye as she and Bill walked the short distance to the room he rented in a quaint house on Main Street.

Saturday morning, jack-o-lanterns frowned or smiled from every store window in downtown Newberry. The cool early morning air gave Virginia a chill and she moved closer to Bill as they walked along the narrow streets. Bill took Virginia to the Lydia Mill, where he had secured employment. The Lydia, although larger than the local mills of Clover, resembled the much smaller textile mills in appearance. They walked further and passed the grounds where the circus had performed the previous weekend. Virginia secretly wished she had arrived earlier and been a part of the audience. Litter still covered the ground and several young boys busied themselves stuffing each piece in burlap bags tied with ropes to their waists.

"Most of the town of Newberry was here last weekend," Bill commented.

"I bet it was pretty exciting," Virginia replied.

"Maybe the next time the circus is here, we'll see it together," Bill remarked.

"I would love that," Virginia answered.

Virginia stopped to read some of the circus posters still evident along the street even though the circus had departed some seven days before. They ducked into a diner on the square filled with young fresh faced students from Newberry College for a bit of lunch before resuming their sight seeing tour. Virginia fell in love with the quaint little town and looked forward to the day when Bill would find a home here for the two of them.

Bill and Virginia spent a quiet Sunday morning together but late in the afternoon Virginia once again found herself on the train bound for Clover. Sadness enveloped her as Bill disappeared from sight. Already, she had begun to anticipate his next letter.

The month of October disappeared before Virginia's eyes. Bill wrote faithfully each week and his letters kept her going. He rode the train to Clover as many weekends as he could afford but Virginia longed to return to Newberry with him each time she waved good-bye. Several attempts at procuring a place for the two of them did not work out and left them both discouraged and disheartened. Available homes had become scarce during depression and this continued as more and more men rode the train into town in search of employment, just as Bill had done.

Virginia rode the train to Newberry in November and joined Bill for Thanksgiving. She had never been away from her family on any holiday but time with Bill was worth the sacrifice.

Bill came home for three days at Christmas and they enjoyed this special time together. Virginia found it hard to share Bill with their friends and family, so treasured was her time with him.

Work in the Lydia Mill began to taper off after Christmas and continued to decline into the New Year. Bill sensed a layoff, possibly only weeks away, and began a search for other work. He wrote Virginia and explained that his time in Newberry might come to a close soon and with it Virginia's dream of a home there. It was the greatest disappointment of all for them because Virginia was pregnant with their first child.

Bill found a job in Lancaster at the local bleachery and for a few more weeks he enjoyed gainful employment. Virginia received a hastily written note from him in late January.

January 23rd
8:30 A.M.

Dearest Pal,

They told me that there isn't any use to come back to The Bleachery any more this week. That's what the boss told me himself. I talked to him at dinner time. Some one said that it looked as if I was having lunch with him. I hardly know what to do. I may see you on Friday or Saturday. I am still seeking a home, a pretty little nest just for me and you and "Little Billy". Well honey, I'll close for now. Write me a long letter.

Always,
Your, Bill

Bill located work in Kershaw, South Carolina the first week of February and Virginia learned of it in a letter dated February 14, 1936, 8 A.M.

Kershaw, S. C.
Wed. Night

Dearest Pal,

I guess you will be glad to hear that I am working again. I'm gold mining to beat the band. I didn't think I was going to get on but they put me to work 12 o'clock today.

I don't know where we can get a place to stay though. I will look out for a place and get one for me and you as soon as I can. I will send you some money when I get straightened out. It won't be much, honey, but it will help out I guess. I am boarding again out here at the mine. As soon as I can buy you some clothes and shoes and get a place for us to stay, I'll be seeing you. I've got lots to tell you when I see you again, honey. I hope you won't mind waiting a little while. I hate to stay away from you. Don't worry because everything will be okay sometime. I hope, pretty soon.

When you write, just send it to Kershaw. I'll get it. I hope to hear from you very soon. I need a long sweet letter from a short sweet gal. I'll write you more next time. I am pretty tired now.

So long, you be sweet and don't worry.

I'll be all,
Your, Bill

Bill's constant absences were hard for Virginia. She continued to work and fill her time with plans for the new baby on the way. Bill's frequent moving around created an unspoken tension between Virginia and her mother. Virginia could see that I- told- you- so look in her mother's eyes but her faith in Bill remained firm and she clung to the hope that she and Bill would be together again soon. She did not mention the baby to her parents. It would only create more distance between her and her mother. The time for this disclosure loomed in the near future as she was already finding it difficult to conceal her extra weight gain. Thomas and Catherine had broken the news at Sunday dinner that they were expecting a baby in September. Although the news was received well by her parents, Virginia realized that it would not be so for her and Bill. Her parents' great concern over Bill's absences and constant wandering would overshadow any hope of their news being accepted with great joy. Virginia remained silent in the matter, penned a letter to Bill, and prayed for a house.

On February 25th, Virginia received a reply to her letter.

Kershaw, South Carolina
Thursday night

Hello Gin,

I received your letter today. I sure was glad to hear from you honey. I thought I would never get it though. This makes three letters to your one. I knew I would hear by Tuesday. I waited as long as I could. So Tuesday night I walked all the way to town and back just for one word from you. But surprised I was. Nothing new though. Looks like I am in for a lot of surprises. I may see you Saturday if I can, sweetheart. I am so lonesome and tired tonight. I feel like I am going to fall to pieces. I haven't found us a place yet. I am going to try and rent a house over here. They are sorry houses but I can't do any better. I don't believe. I am going to do the best I can.

I am still working, hun. I'm staying at the same place. There is not anything to me anymore except dreams for us.

So long old pal, be good and don't worry. I'll always be

Your,
Bill

Bill rode the train home on Saturday and he and Virginia spent a couple days together. He stayed with her in her parents' home and tension ran high. Bill understood their coolness and concern for Virginia and dreaded the thought of revealing the news of Virginia's pregnancy. But both realized that the secret could not be kept any longer. They broke the news at Sunday dinner. It was not received well and for the first time Bill couldn't wait to board a bus for Kershaw. The distance between him and Virginia's parents grew even greater.

Chapter 12

The tension between Virginia and her parents continued into the ensuing week and time seemed at a standstill. Catherine came to visit her sister often and these visits afforded some relief to Virginia. She and Thomas offered much encouragement and were genuinely excited about the baby. Virginia and Catherine shared some lighthearted teasing of each other concerning their expanding waistlines and the laughter lifted the melancholy that plagued Virginia. But when the laughter faded away, Catherine's voice took on a more serious note.

"Things will work out fine, Virginia. Just you wait and see," Catherine said. "Bill will find a place for you and the baby soon and all this will be behind you. Don't let Mother and Daddy get you down."

"It's easy for you to say," Virginia replied. "You don't have to live with them apart from Thomas."

"I know," Catherine replied. "But just hold on a little longer."

Daniel and Anna Jane came frequently to get Virginia out of the house. These outings proved a much needed diversion for Virginia and she anticipated them with eagerness.

Virginia's job at Mr. Oren's was a godsend as she waited for news from Bill. Several days passed before the postman delivered a letter that bore a postmark of March 3rd, 3:30 p.m., the first one since Bill boarded the train Sunday past.

Kershaw, South Carolina
Monday night

Dearest Girl,

I write to let you know that I had a devil of a time getting here last night. I caught a bus about five minutes after I left you and went to Rock Hill. I was most sure to catch a bus there but I couldn't. I had to thumb it on in. That's my luck you know. I had to walk from Heath Springs to Kershaw. I got here about 9:p.m. It was worth it though just to see you. I sure was glad to be with my pal and what little time I could. I enjoyed it just like I did when we were sporting. The only part I hated was the leaving part. I sure hated to leave you, Gin. I hope you are not like your Bill, not in much heart for anything. Of course I feel better this week than I did the week before I saw you. It helped me a lot and I hope it helped you.

I am going to try to get a place for us as soon as I possibly can. I want us to be together more than ever. This can't last always. I hope. If I can get a place this week, I am going to start our little home this week. This is how quick I want to start. We are going to be okay. Don't worry. I will do all I can. I am looking ahead for better times for you and me. The good master will take care of us all through the years to come. Sorry that the news about the baby did not go over well. We expected as much though. All will be well.

I will turn in now. Write soon and remember I love you Gin.

I'll always be only,
Your, Bill

Bill caught the bus from Kershaw to Clover on Saturday morning. Virginia waited for him at the bus depot on Main Street. The cool March air held a faint promise of spring as Virginia drew her coat tighter around her expanding middle. Bill waved from the window as the bus came to a stop and Virginia returned the wave and smiled.

"Right on time," Bill said as he held Virginia in his arms.

"Daniel and Anna Jane are waiting for us in the diner," Virginia commented.

"Let's go," Bill replied.

Daniel motioned to Virginia and Bill as they entered the diner.

"Good to see you, Bill," Daniel commented as Virginia and Bill slid into the booth with them.

"Same here," Bill replied.

"How are things in Kershaw?" Daniel inquired.

"Not good, not good," Bill answered. "Always short on work and can't be certain how long this will even last."

"I think it's the same most everywhere right now," Daniel said.

Bill and Virginia stayed the night with Daniel and Anna Jane. Bill did not care for another weekend with Virginia's parents and it was a comfort to be with old friends.

Bill and Virginia went to the local movie to see *Call of the Wild.* Virginia tried to keep her mind distracted from the thought of Bill's departure in so short a time. After the movie, she walked with him to the train depot. They spoke of their plans for a future together and Virginia held hope in her heart that they were not just dreams. The sight of the train as it pulled up in front of them filled Virginia with dread. Bill promised to write and boarded the train. After a quick wave good-bye from the window, Bill disappeared from sight.

The old familiar loneliness swirled around Virginia and for the first time, a small part of her began to loose faith in Bill.

Almost a week passed and Virginia did not hear any word from Bill. The waiting was endless for her. Too little conversation passed between her and her mother these days and added to her loneliness. Virginia tried to keep busy and distract herself from the problems that seemed to surround her. Thomas and Catherine came over on Sunday for dinner and shared some time with Virginia. As was his custom, Thomas made much jest over the advanced size of the two sisters and the room echoed with their laughter.

The postman left a letter from Bill on Thursday. The wait had been hard for Virginia. The letter was postmarked Kershaw, March 5th, 8 a.m.

> *Kershaw, South Carolina*
> *Sunday*

Dear Sweetheart,

It is now 2 o'clock. This time last Sunday I was getting ready to leave my pal to be so lonesome and blue as I am today. I sure wish I could have been with you this past weekend. I enjoy every minute that I spend with you. It is my greatest desire to be with you. I pray that you are well. All I have is the blues.

Honey, I talked to a man about a house and he said he thought I could get a house by the end of next week. He told me yesterday he would let me know on Wednesday. As soon as I get a house, I will let you know. I don't want you to think I am not trying. There is only one thing that I can do and that is to wait until I can get a house close to my work. I want us to start housekeeping as soon as you do yourself, Pal, and you know I am. If I don't pretty soon, remember that I will be seeing you soon anyway. It is doggone lonesome without my Gin. It won't be long now. We will be okay before long. I always have hope and don't believe I will be fooled.

I don't want you to worry and cry your little self to death. That is not the way to take it. Remember, you are not a girl now. You are a grown up lady and ladies like you don't want to play babies anymore. Darling, I will write soon.

Your,
Bill

P.S. Write soon.

Virginia folded the letter and placed it in the antique box on her dresser. Her asthma had returned with a vengeance and the difficulty in breathing resulted in a lack of energy. She stretched out on the bed and fell into an exhausted sleep.

The next few days were unpleasant for Virginia and the asthma showed no mercy. Dr. McGill prescribed more of the small yellow pills which offered some relief but left Virginia jittery and irritable.

Bill letters arrived frequently but he was unable to visit in Clover for the next three weekends. He chose instead to squirrel away any money he could for the house they hoped to have. Virginia answered Bill's letters faithfully and tried to keep a good face on things. But Bill sensed her deep loneliness in his absence. He grabbed any available work and held on fiercely to hope.

Virginia made no mention of her illness to Bill. She saw no reason to burden him further with things already at such a low point. She would tell him in due time.

Virginia and Catherine spent more and more time together. The wages from her work at Mr. Oren's allowed Virginia to buy a few things for the baby and her outings with Catherine, over time, became more and more treasured to her. But as busy as Virginia was, loneliness continued to be a faithful companion. Even the frequent letters from Bill did not dissuade it.

Virginia received a letter in late March with a postmark of Kershaw, March 26th, 3:30 p.m. The letter read

Kershaw, South Carolina
Wednesday, P.M.

Dearest Pal,

I received your letter today and was glad to hear from you. I am sorry you have been sick sweetheart. I am awful sorry you didn't care enough about me to let me know sooner. That's a pretty howdy do. Honey, I trust you are better by now. I hate for my pal to be sick. Hope you will be well by Saturday and Sunday as I plan to see you then. I wouldn't have been away like this if I could have helped it. It just couldn't be helped. It is hard for me to explain with you there and me here. You just don't realize what all I have been through. You know some of it but not all. As much as you worry now, I don't know what would happen if you knew everything.

Well, I will stop arguing on this paper. That's the only way I can argue and I can't do without that you know.

This will be the last letter you get from me before I see you unless something happens. Look for me Saturday or Sunday. Don't worry about anything.

Remember, I love you and I wait (not patiently) for you.

Always your,
Bill

Saturday morning, Virginia walked to the bus depot. The chill of early March disappeared on the March winds. The warmth of the sun pleased Virginia and renewed her hope for new beginnings. The bus arrived on time and Bill bounded off with a wide smile on his face.

"Gin," he said with an unusual excitement in his voice. "We have us a house. It's the one I wrote you about. I just found out yesterday."

"Bill, I can't believe it." Virginia said.

"It's not much of a house but it's close to my work and we can be together." Bill continued. "Gin, leave with me tomorrow afternoon."

"Of course," Virginia answered. "This is all I've been waiting for."

Chapter 13

Kershaw in 1936 was typical of most small southern towns. It, also, had joined in the struggle of the depression. Its three textile mills barely hung on and its workers earned their living with the threat of the same work shortages, wage cuts, and lay offs that plagued textile mills throughout the South. Virginia found the town agreeable but lacking in the appeal of the quaint town of Newberry. The white frame house they moved into stood two blocks from the Haw Mill where Bill worked. Virginia did everything she knew to make it as attractive as possible within their modest budget. Most every convenience was within walking distance and she enjoyed brief walks to the grocery store against Bill's better judgment. The fact that they had yet to contact a doctor in Kershaw for Virginia caused great concern for Bill even though the asthma that tormented her the past few weeks had loosened it hold. Bill hoped the improvement would continue until they saved enough money to pay for a doctor's care. Bill and Virginia made friends with a couple who lived next door, Ralph and Lydia Wallace. Ralph worked in the mill with Bill and they walked to work together each morning. Virginia welcomed

Lydia's company while Bill was at work. Lydia was the mother of a six month old infant and from her Virginia learned as much as she could about the care of an infant. Lydia's presence gave Bill some relief from his concern for Virginia. She appeared to be a responsible young woman with a level head and Bill was grateful for the friendship that developed between them. At least once a week they all got together at Ralph and Lydia's for a good card game, reminiscent of the card games they once shared with Daniel and Anna Jane.. Bill and Virginia were in agreement that these were the best of days.

The last week of April, Bill was halfway through his shift at work. An uneasy feeling had accompanied him on his walk to work earlier that morning and had not abated even in the midst of his busy day. Virginia's health improved enough that Bill relaxed his concern and seldom allowed it to consume his mind to the degree it once had. Instead, he focused on the fact that he and Virginia were together, something that they both at times thought would never happen. Work remained steady and relieved some of Bill's financial woes enough that he could focus on the arrival of the new baby with some relief.

When Bill left to begin his shift at the mill, Virginia started her morning in the usual round of housework. She wanted her house in order because she knew Lydia and the baby were to spend the day with her. About mid- morning, Virginia felt a slight tightening in her chest. She walked out onto the porch for a breath of fresh air and hoped that the asthma wouldn't return to torment her once more. She noticed Lydia pushing the baby carriage up the street and remained on the porch until their arrival. Lydia noticed the look of concern on Virginia's face and asked, "Virginia, do you feel okay?"

"I'm alright, just a little tightness in my chest." Virginia answered.

"Let's stay out here on the porch for a while," Lydia said.

The fresh air offered little relief to Virginia and she returned inside. Lydia propped several pillows under her head as she rested on the bed. When Virginia's breathing became more labored, Lydia's concern increased.

"Virginia, I think I need to go get Bill." Lydia commented.

"No, Bill needs to work and I shouldn't trouble him," Virginia answered. "Let's wait a while before you do that."

Lydia continued to sit beside the bed until Virginia's breathing became alarmingly labored.

"I'm going to the mill to get Bill," Lydia said rising from her chair. "I'll take the baby with me and we'll be back in no time."

Unable to answer, Virginia shook her head in a definitive acknowledgement. Lydia caught the anxiousness in her eyes.

The noise in the mill was deafening as Lydia tried to convey to Bill the urgency of Virginia's situation.

"Bill, Virginia needs you at home." she breathlessly shouted to him. "She's in the midst of a severe asthma attack. I've done everything I know to do but nothing seems to help."

Bill did not speak a word but grabbed Lydia by the arm and they hurried out of the mill toward home.

Virginia sat upright in a chair and struggled for breath as Lydia and Bill entered the house. The look on Bill's face conveyed his concern for her.

"Virginia," he said. "Do you have any of the medication that Dr. McGill prescribed for you? You must have some somewhere."

Virginia shook her head, no.

"Are you sure?" Bill asked as he headed for the chair in the bedroom where Virginia always left her handbag.

He emptied the contents of the handbag on the bed and searched frantically for the familiar brown bottle of pills. When he didn't see it, he walked over to the chest of drawers and began to empty them of all the clothing. Finally, he came across the pink bed-jacket Virginia's mother had given her before Dr. McGill's last visit at their home. He fumbled in the pink satin pocket of the bed jacket until he felt some small tablets in the bottom. He pulled them out and held in his hand the familiar yellow tablets that would bring Virginia some relief.

Bill ran to the kitchen, filled a glass of water, and returned to Virginia. He sat beside the chair until Virginia's breathing became less labored, the medicine haven taken its desired effect.

Lydia could see that Bill was still visibly upset when he turned to say, "Thanks Lydia, for all you've done. I don't know what would've happened without all your help."

Lydia sat with Bill and Virginia until Virginia slept a peaceful sleep. Then, satisfied that the crisis was over, she and the baby returned home.

Later in the evening, Virginia stirred from her rest and Bill prepared a light supper for both of them. Bill's silence conveyed to Virginia that much lay heavy on his mind.

"Bill," Virginia began. "I'm sorry about today."

"Aw, it's not your fault," Bill answered. "I just feel so helpless when you're sick."

"I'd say you knew just what to do this afternoon," Virginia replied.

"You just don't realize how frightened I was for you," Bill answered.

"It's frightening for me too," Virginia continued.

"Virginia, I've been thinking that maybe the place for you right now with a baby on the way and the asthma and all, is in Clover with your family. Dr. McGill takes good care of you and he's only minutes away."

"But Bill, I don't want to leave now. We're happy here and I don't want to separate from you. Lydia is close by and I'll be okay," Virginia begged.

"It's not fair to put this burden on Lydia. The baby is enough for her to handle right now," Bill continued.

"I guess you're right," Virginia answered.

"I don't think I could stand another scare like today. Maybe, if you return to Clover until after the baby comes both of you could come back here as soon as the baby is old enough. I'm just worried, Virginia, that something might go wrong with you or the baby and with no extra money for doctor visits who knows what might happen? You need to be closer to your family and under Dr. McGill's care at a time like this," Bill reasoned.

"I know you're right," Virginia replied. "But I just can't stand the thought of leaving you here alone."

"It won't be long before the baby is born. It'll be hard but you'll be better off for right now," Bill said.

"Alright, Bill," Virginia answered as tears glistened on her cheeks.

Part 111
Return to Clover

Chapter 14

On a rainy Saturday morning, the following weekend, Bill and Virginia rode the train to Clover. The rain mimicked their mood and added further gloom to the situation. Bill stayed with Virginia throughout the weekend and helped to get things in order before he boarded the train once more on Sunday afternoon. Virginia did not accompany him to the depot but chose instead to remain with her parents. The thought of Bill's departure without her rendered Virginia a tough blow and she did not relish watching the train carry him away once again.

The rain broke early on Monday morning and Virginia heard Bertha's familiar humming as she ambled up the walk. Virginia's mother waited for Bertha in the doorway and led her into the bedroom where Virginia lay in the bed propped up on two huge pillows.

"Lordy, Lordy," Bertha said. "Miss Virginia, are you back here in Clover so soon? Don't you worry about anything; Bertha will help take care of you and the baby. Don't you fret any, you hear?"

"I'll be alright," Virginia replied.

"Sure you will," Bertha answered and flashed a big smile exposing the gold teeth she was so proud of. "You just let Bertha take care of you."

Bertha straightened the bed and plumped the pillows for Virginia's head, all the while strutting about the room like an old mother hen.

A few days later, Thomas dropped Catherine by for a visit with Virginia. They spent much of their time together caught up in a discussion about their advancing pregnancies. Catherine and Thomas devoted a tiny spare bedroom in their home to the baby and painstakingly painted it a pale yellow. The white organdy curtains hanging from the windows gave the room a light airy effect.

Virginia made plans to use her own bedroom for her baby. The room, already a soft color of green, required no painting and the colors in the curtains lent themselves to either a girl or boy. The tiny cradle that she and Catherine had once used already sat expectantly in the corner of the room. Bill placed it there after retrieving it from the attic. Catherine's visit diverted Virginia's mind from Bill's absence and all the trouble that seemed to seek them out.

Late in the afternoon, Dr. McGill dropped in to check on Virginia and dissuade her of any idea that her asthma would impart an ill effect on the baby.

"Virginia," Dr. McGill said. "There is no need for you to be concerned about the baby. Everything is as it should be and you'll have a perfectly healthy child. You just get the proper amount of rest and stop your worrying."

"I'll try," Virginia answered.

Virginia did as Dr. McGill suggested and due to her mother's help and Bertha's constant doting, her health improved. Time passed swiftly and before long Mr. Parks dropped a letter from Bill in the mail box. The letter was post- marked May 14th, 1936 and Virginia was swift to open it and read.

Kershaw
1:45 Thursday A.M.

Dearest Gin,

As I am very lonesome and have nothing to do but sleep, I will try and write to let you know that I have not received a letter from you since I left you in Clover. I sure have been looking for one since though. I am worried to death about you, Gin. Get sick and don't write to me will you? It's not my fault this time. I have asked about mail ever since Monday past. I guess everything is alright though because if you wanted to hear from me you would write. If you don't have the stamps, let me know. I would have tried to call but I don't have one red cent this week.

This morning is sure another one of those beautiful ones. The moon has just come up and boy is she red. A big cloud is right there over it. I sure wish I had you here with me to look at it.

I am on at night again this week. I live in the hope that I may come to see you one day soon. Anyway, I want you to come home. Do ask Dr. McGill if he thinks it will be alright. It would tickle me to death for you to come home but it may be best for you to stay there until everything is over. It's an awful long trip anyway.

When I get off this morning, it will make 36 hours for me. I put a cement floor in Mr. Sherrill's chicken house yesterday. Of course, I could make day and night for weeks like this, with nothing to do. I haven't heard a thing about us having anything to do soon.

Well, I've about given out of conversation so I will stop until morning. Maybe, I will get a letter. I will write more then.

Thursday P.M.

Well Dearest,

I still look for mail but I never get any. Sweetheart, please let me know what's wrong at once. I can't stand this. Write something if it's not but three words. I am crazy to know why you haven't written to me. I try to think that it's the company's fault but it has been so long and I ask them every day. Just think about it. I haven't heard from you since I left you on Sunday.

If I had a way to go to town, I might get this letter off this evening but I don't know whether I can or not. I will try to because if you are as anxious to hear from me as I am you, I know you are standing on your head.

Well, I will close because I am so worried I can't write.

Your,
Bill

Virginia placed the letter back in the envelope and grabbed a pen from the dresser drawer and hastily penned a letter to Bill. She sealed the letter and placed it inside the mailbox for Mr. Parks to pick up the following morning.

Four days later, Bill received Virginia's letter. Eagerly he opened it and his eyes fell upon Virginia's neat handwriting.

Clover, South Carolina
Monday, May 16ᵗʰ

Hello Bill,

Gee, I would love to see you because I am so blue and feel so bad. If you were only here, I would be okay. I hope it won't be long before I see you again because every day away from you gets worse and worse. I don't know if I can stand it much longer.

Well dear, I guess you will find out something about your job today. I hope things work out for you. I am praying that it will because the sweetest place in the world, dear, would be to be at home with you. If things don't work out though, don't give up. I know it is hard for us to be away from each other but sweetheart, we all have our ups and downs. Don't look on the dark side of life because the clouds will soon roll by. We'll be okay some ole day as long as we have each other. I'll stick with you, Bill, when the whole world turns you down.

Bill, I guess you are mad because I haven't written but this is the best I could do. I couldn't write before now. I will tell you about it when I see you. Please answer real soon. Hurry and come home because I need you.

Your,
Gin

At a minimum of once a week, Catherine and Thomas came by to visit and they often went to a movie together. Some nights, they joined each other for a meal at the local diner. Virginia's asthma improved and she settled into the daily routine of her parents' home. She wrote Bill more often and made plans to join him in Kershaw for a weekend. Bill gave the house up and moved into a large Victorian home owned by a Mr. John Sherrill. Mr. Sherrill rented rooms to the mill workers and two other men, Fred Benfield and Archie Grissom also occupied rooms there. Bill enjoyed the company of the two men as the house had become too quiet after Virginia's return to Clover.

Two weeks later, Virginia traveled on the train to Kershaw. Bill had sent her the money for the ticket and Dr. McGill reluctantly gave his permission for the trip.

"Virginia, you know you shouldn't travel, you carrying a baby and all," her mother admonished.

"If Dr. McGill says its okay, then its okay," Virginia replied as she packed her suitcase. "Anyway, Bill will take good care of me."

Chapter 15

M r. Sherrill lived in a rambling Victorian home about two blocks from the Haw Mill. His twenty year old daughter, Susan, lived in the house also and helped with the house-keeping and cooking. Her mother, June, had passed a few years back. In the following years, she and her father had become very close. Bill mentioned Susan from time to time but just how attractive she really was came as a surprise to Virginia and the ease with which she and Bill interacted made her uneasy. Virginia found it a comfort to know that Susan was engaged to a man named Ted Smith, a friendly man with a wide grin that displayed a mouth full of perfectly aligned teeth. He also worked in the Haw Mill, rented a room in a boarding house across town, and was a frequent guest in Mr. Sherrill's home.

Saturday night, Bill, Virginia, and Susan caught a cab to meet Ted at the local diner. Ted entertained everyone with his impersonations of the most famous movie stars of the day and Susan chimed in with a few of her own. They were soon joined by some friends Bill had made at the mill. They laughed and joked well into the night and Virginia found rest from the worry that had consumed her in the last few weeks.

On Sunday morning, Bill and Virginia attended the quaint Methodist church that Mr. Sherrill and Susan attended regularly. Mr. Sherrill and his wife, June, had married in this church thirty years before and it was in the cemetery behind the church that June now resided with other members of her family.

After lunch, Bill and Virginia sat in the oversized swing on the front porch of the house. The porch wrapped openly around the house and enabled the cool breeze to carry with it the sweet smell of the honeysuckle vines that clung to the hedges surrounding the house. It added a sweet, soothing aroma to a peaceful afternoon. Virginia longed for the day to last and was certain she would often visit the memory of these rare hours together.

Late in the afternoon, Virginia boarded the train once more and returned to Clover. Thomas and Catherine waited for her at the depot upon her arrival and made small talk as they traveled along.

"Hope it won't be long before you and Bill see one another again. This must be hard for you both," Catherine commented. "This will all be behind you as soon as the baby comes. It won't be that much longer."

"I know," Virginia replied. "But it seems like an eternity to us right now."

Virginia kept herself as busy as possible in the ensuing days. The nursery was complete now and when Bill could, he sent money to purchase a few essential items for the baby. It wasn't much but it was enough to get by for a while.

The sultry summer temperatures of the South accompanied the arrival of June. The added weight of Virginia's pregnancy made it difficult for her find relief from the oppressive heat. After lunch each day, she sought comfort in front of the fan Bertha had placed in her bedroom. But she cherished above all, the cool evening breezes that wafted across the porch. She wrote Bill more often even though her life seldom deviated from the busy routine of each day. She understood just how much her letters meant to Bill.

Almost two weeks after Virginia's return from Kershaw, Mr. Parks dropped a letter postmarked Kershaw, June 6th, 1936 in the mailbox. Virginia reclined on the bed to catch the cooling breeze of the fan and began to read.

Kershaw, South Carolina
Monday, P.M.

Dearest Darling,

Today is a very nice day to write letters so I will answer the one I just received from you a little while ago. I was more than anxious to know how you were getting along. I worry a lot about your being far away from me. I hope you are doing better and not worrying yourself to death.

I guess its getting pretty hot on you now. It is awful warm here today. I am back on daytime again for this week. Maybe I will catch up with my sleep now. It has been so hot until a body couldn't sleep in daytime.

We sure have been having it here. The whole shebang almost had war here Saturday, another one of the Faulkenburrys gone. Haskall Faulkenburry and Mr. Sherrill had a little push and pull fight and Mr.Sherrill ran him out of the office. Oscar has to move off the place and I am looking for mine to come any minute. It wouldn't surprise me at anytime. I guess they understand the shape I am in at the present and that's the reason they keep me on. I really don't believe this place will ever do any more good. You can't ever tell.

Well, honey, I guess I had better find a stopping place because it is almost mail time.

Don't worry about anything and when the time comes, please let me know. I don't expect I can see you anymore before that time. I didn't draw a cent Saturday. They took it all.

Your, beloved,
Bill

Virginia jotted a few lines to Bill in response to his letter and tried to get in a short nap.

Four days later, Virginia received another letter, a letter of urgency from Bill.

Kershaw, June 8th, 1936
Wednesday

Dearest Gin,

I will change the topic today. This is a letter of both business and concern. What I need this time is if at anytime I can get hold of Shorty Straton's truck or any other please let me know at once.

Understand that I am not out of a job yet but I am about ready to get out until I find out what they are going to do .I talked to Mr. Sherrill yesterday and he said I would be okay if I could get work somewhere else. I can get my job back here anytime I want in case the mill starts back up.

I tried to borrow the money for you yesterday but I couldn't get it. He said what money he had in the bank was only $6.00 and he *has given checks on part of it. If I can't get up $10.00 Saturday, I will send you the seven I know I will get. If you happen not to need it before a couple weeks, I can pay the rest. I will try to get the money as soon as possible. I could have gotten it yesterday. He had it. What goes out of here comes out of his pocket. He cannot loan the company's money.*

I've got to do better than I am doing so if you see a chance of a job anywhere let me know as soon as possible.

I just received your letter yesterday afternoon. When the time comes, I will be there. Don't be worrying and crying. Everything will be okay. I know it will.

This leaves me on the job and feeling like something the cat drug in. I went frog hunting last night and didn't get in until eleven o'clock.

Write soon and tell me all about everything. If you have to, write a check on me and get it cashed. I'll get more money somehow.

Your,
Bill

Over in the afternoon, Daniel and Anna Jane came by to check on Virginia as they promised Bill they would do. Virginia relayed to them all the information Bill had conveyed in his last letter. Daniel assured Virginia that he would procure Shorty Straton's truck in case Bill felt a need for it. The duration of the evening, they spent in general conversation. Virginia enjoyed their company and it helped to make the night a little shorter and kinder. As soon as Daniel and Anna Jane departed, Virginia grabbed a sheet of paper and penned a letter to Bill. She informed him of Daniel's kind offer of the truck and willingness to help in the event that he needed to make a move. She felt the void that being apart had created between them since her move back home and feared that the loss of employment for Bill might further add to the strain. She sealed the letter and placed it in the mailbox for Mr. Parks to pick up.

Work at the Haw Mill continued to decline and Bill saw the writing on the wall. He began to search for other work in the hope that as things got back to normal at the mill he could return. But with the birth of the baby imminent and Virginia's health problems, Bill realized he must keep a steady income of some fashion.

Two weeks later, Bill found a job, of sorts, in an ore mine there in Kershaw. Daniel and two of his friends from work showed up in Kershaw with Shorty Stratton's truck to help Bill move from Mr. Sherrill's. Bill hated to leave but room and board closer to his new job demanded it. By the time Daniel arrived with the truck, Bill had sold the last of the household items, he and Virginia had acquired in the brief time they lived together, leaving few things to load into the truck. In doing so, a sinking feeling consumed Bill and imparted an uncomfortable emotion of finality. He could only hope that this emotion was just that, an emotion, and not in any way a forewarning of things to come.

The work in the mine proved hard for Bill and the hours just as difficult. He and Virginia continued to write each other frequently. The due date for the birth of the baby loomed just a few weeks away and Bill was growing increasingly anxious. Any word from Virginia was more than welcomed.

Chapter 16

Virginia fared well in her parents' home and at this stage of the pregnancy residing there gave her a sense of much needed security. As hard as she fought against it, she had to admit that Bill was right about her return to Clover. Dr. McGill made two stops a week now to check on her and as far as her health everything looked fine. Bertha showed up more often and tended to her every whim.

"Lawsy me, Miss Virginia, you're as fat as a pig. Looks to me like you carrying three babies," Bertha teased Virginia. "Gonna need lots of help with all those babies; might have to show up here more if you do."

Virginia welcomed Bertha's visits and secretly hoped that she would be present for the birth.

"Wild horses won't keep Bertha away once this baby arrives," Virginia thought.

The first week in July, Virginia received a letter from Bill displaying a postmark date of July 1st. Bill's unhappiness with the job in the mine was evident in the tone of his letters. It was Virginia's hope that since a few weeks had passed, he might have a better outlook about it. Maybe she would get the answer to that in the letter she held.

Kershaw, S.C.
Thursday night

Dearest Virginia,

As I am worrying and wondering how you are tonight, I will write and see if you will answer this one as prompt as you did the last one. I sure would love to hear a little something from you once in a while, honey. As for myself, it is raining and it looks as if I am going to enjoy a rainy night. I am glad to see it rain because it has been so hot here until I have started going naked. Yes sir, I am as red as an Indian.

I would have written to you before now but I have been trying to wait until I got an answer from the last one. I wish you would write more often because I worry about you especially in a time like this.

I guess you are looking for the explosion to break forth for the 4th. If it does I guess you will have something to celebrate or have a grand way to do it. Anyway, I don't suppose it will be much longer. I know that it shouldn't be. I will be almost as glad when it's over as you and I know you will.

I do not know anymore about the mine now than I did before. Only, I don't think it will run too much longer. I will tell you also that I don't like much having a hate of this. I sure don't like the job with the work punched out of it.

Well, I will be expecting a long sweet letter from you pretty soon. Be good and don't worry. I will be home soon.

Your,
Bill

Within three weeks, the Haw Mill came to a complete standstill. As much as Bill disliked the mine, he had succeeded in keeping himself in a steady paycheck. He continued to send Virginia what money he could and pondered how long they could survive in the current situation before it began to erode their relationship. The stresses of the past two years consumed him and left behind more insecurity as to what the future held for the three of them. He couldn't imagine his life without Virginia. He already felt the frustration in Virginia's letters and sensed her disappointment in the situation. Bill wrote more often to cheer her up but he secretly wondered how long it might be before one or both of them just simply gave up and allowed their problems to come between them. Bill prayed that the time together was all that they would loose.

The morning of July 14th broke hot and muggy. Mr. Parks handed a letter from Bill to Virginia as she sat in the oversized rocker on the porch.

"Gonna be a hot one today," Mr. Parks commented.

"Looks like it might," replied Virginia as she reached for the letter.

"Gonna try to finish my route early today. I can't stand this kind of heat," Mr. Parks added.

As Mr. Parks turned to walk away, Virginia noticed the Dalton brothers, Clyde and Lyle, walking along the sidewalk toward town. Their return to Clover did not impart pleasure to many people in town. As they passed, Virginia exchanged a greeting with them. She noticed how their appearance had changed since their departure after the fire at the church. They were taller now and carried themselves with the gait of more mature young men. Virginia hoped that their maturity wasn't just in appearance but

113

also in a deeper maturity that might benefit their future actions. Her mind wandered back over the past two years. Replete with change, the years had brought many turns and twists since she first met Bill at the church picnic. Virginia gave a long sigh and opened the letter.

Kershaw, South Carolina
July 11th, 1936
Friday night

Hello Gin,

I am writing this evening to let you know I am thinking of you. I wonder how you are. I sure hope you are doing better because I worry about you being sick. I would love to see you. If you need anything, please let me know. I can't read your mind way down here.

I am on the job now. The sun is setting but it is still terribly hot. I am about to melt down. I guess it is pretty tough for you now. I haven't slept but one hour at daytime this week. I have caught a few at night though. I have had plenty pretty nights this week. I see the ole moon every night. I will be gone in a couple more nights. You are missing all the turtle doves and whip-o-wills. They are taking the country over. I am to the point that I can call them up in the evening. I called a dove up just a few minutes ago.

How are all the folks? Tell them all hello for ole Bill. I guess you and sis look so much alike they can't tell you apart by now.

Well, everything is going along smooth now but I can hardly stay here. I need more work or excitement or both. This is a devil of a place to sit and brood all night or day. I sure wish the Hawthorne would start hiring soon. Well, I suppose things will be okay someday.

I will close now because I know nothing much to tell you this time, Pal. There is one thing I want to tell you. Take everything as best you can do. That is all you can do. Don't worry yourself to death either, that is if you haven't already. I will be home when you send for me. So long and be good.

Your, Bill

Virginia folded the letter and added it to the others in the box on her dresser. She stretched out on the bed and the hum of the fan lulled her into a deep sleep.

An hour later, Virginia woke to the familiar voices of her Uncle Erwin and Aunt Erline. Virginia enjoyed their company and welcomed the distraction from her melancholy mood. Daisy, their young daughter, accompanied them and her presence pleased Virginia. Daisy was a bright child with a happy disposition and an inquisitive mind. Virginia found it refreshing to have the young girl around.

The hot summer days drug by for Virginia. She confined herself to the house now and busied herself with the mundane tasks of the household. She found herself increasingly anxious about the impending birth and more than a little apprehensive about her relationship with Bill.

A letter from Bill arrived on July 30th, postmarked July 21, 1936, Kershaw, South Carolina.

Kershaw, S. C.
Monday night

Dearest Pal,

I received your letter Friday but this is the first chance I have had to write. I am sorry I didn't get to see you Saturday but I couldn't get off. I had planned to surprise you but my plans fell through. The water pump here tore up Friday night and we didn't get it fixed until Saturday evening. It looks as if I will wait until the moon fulls again. Isn't that when most babies are born? I will have to wait until Saturday now or borrow some money one. I know you are anxious to see the baby as I am also. We will just have to wait a little longer.

The moon sure has been pretty. It was awful pretty last night. I watched last night as I am back on at night this week. I wish I could see you. I suppose I will see you this weekend if you don't send for me before.

Well, I don't have much news this time. In fact, I don't feel a bit good. Don't worry though because I am not sick.

It is almost mail time. I will write more next time.

Write soon and let me know how you are about everything.

Be good and don't worry. I still love you.

Always,
Your, Bill

Part IV
Motherhood

Chapter 17

Just before midnight on August 9th, Daniel heard a knock on his door. Groggy with sleep, he peeked through the blinds to see Mr. Nivens at the door. Daniel slipped the lock back on the door and opened it.

"Daniel," Mr. Nivens spoke. "You better go after Bill. Virginia's time has come."

"I'll leave right away," Daniel answered. "Is there anything else we can do?"

"No," Mr. Nivens replied. "Her mama is with her now and Dr. McGill is on the way. I'm on my way now to get Bertha."

"Alright then," Bill answered as Mr. Nivens turned to leave. "Tell Virginia that I'll have Bill there in no time."

Daniel arrived at the boarding house where Bill lived just before dawn. Bill, just rising for his shift at the mine, wasted no time in getting in the car with Daniel.

Daniel and Bill arrived in plenty of time before the birth of the baby. Bill was allowed to sit beside Virginia and hold her hand for a brief time before the pains became more intense and Bertha insisted that he leave the room.

"You can't do anything more in here, Mr. Bill," Bertha said. "Let the doctor do his work now and I'll let you know when the baby comes. Bertha won't let anything happen to those two. You can count on it. No sir. They'll be just fine."

Bill reluctantly left the room.

Janet Leanne Blackmon entered the world on August 10th at 4.00 p.m. Bertha kept her word and told Bill immediately of the baby's birth. Bill jumped up as she entered the room.

"You have a fine baby girl, eyes as blue as a robin's eggs," Bertha announced. "Yes sir. A fine baby girl, just what Bertha wanted."

Bill chuckled at Bertha as he left the room to meet his daughter for the first time.

Bill stayed with Daniel and Anna Jane for the following two nights and filled his days with Virginia and his new daughter. These were the happiest days for him in quite some time. Late on Sunday afternoon, he boarded the train for Kershaw.

Virginia gained most of her strength back within a week, thanks to the help she received from her mother and Bertha. The baby flourished under Bertha's careful watch and time flew by. Ten days vanished before Virginia realized how long Bill had been gone. The postmark on the letter Mr. Parks dropped in the mailbox drew her attention to the passage of time and she quickly opened the letter to read

Kershaw, S C.
Tuesday A.M.

Dear Sweetheart,
I haven't heard from you yet but I guess I will sometime. I am writing just the same so to keep you from worrying.

Did you get the money I sent you, Gin? I sent a money order last week and a check followed that. If you didn't, let me know. How are you and Janet, honey? I hope you both are fine.

Gin, I want you to see Dr. McGill or get someone else to tell him I said to write out a statement saying the baby is okay. I have to have it so I can get the insurance policy on Janet. The policy is here so do that and mail it back this week if you can. I want it by Saturday.

I sure would love to see Janet and hold her once more. I love you both.

Gin, they say a new mine will start up before long now. I don't know much about it but I do know they are getting ready to do something. They are doing a heck of a lot of work here. I sure will be glad if they do start and raise wages. They are not going to run this mill any longer, they say. I am back on at night again. It looks as if they want to put both shifts on me. That would suite me okay if I get the other dollar.

I am still watching the moon, honey. It is about gone but I see it every night. It sure is pretty. It is also lonesome without you, Gin. When do you think you can come back to Kershaw? Please write and tell me. I will be after you. You know I want you home, darling. In fact, I didn't really want you to leave me here all alone.

Well, I will stop and write more next time. I am short on news this time, sweetheart. Write soon. Be good. Don't worry. Kiss my baby for me!

Lots of love for you and Janet,

Your, Bill

The month of August became a blur to Virginia. The baby kept everyone busy and a constant stream of friends and family came to view the infant child. Virginia, caught up in the business of each day, grew lax in replying to Bill's letters. By the time each day drew to a close and night fell, she slept exhausted in the bed. She received the money order and the cash that Bill mentioned in his last letter and gave a portion of it to Dr. McGill as Bill had instructed. Dr. McGill in turn filled out the paper Bill requested to purchase the life insurance policy. Virginia was swift in dropping it in the mail for Bill. She made some plans to look for a job as soon as her health would allow it. The money Bill was able to send was hardly enough now and she wanted to relieve him of any strain she possibly could. Bill's absence seldom crossed her mind now, so full was her life with the baby.

Catherine visited often to help with the baby. It proved perfect training for her with her baby due in less than a month. Virginia basked in all the attention lavished on her and the baby.

Bill rode the train to Clover in mid August to spend the weekend. On Saturday night, Virginia left the baby in the care of her mother so that she and Bill might join Daniel and Anna Jane for a quick meal and a movie. Virginia was eager for the time away from the baby and the past month of confinement at home. Throughout the evening, Bill sensed coolness between him and Virginia but he couldn't reconcile this feeling with any particular problem between the two of them. Thinking it might be the stress of the baby's birth and all the activity that followed, he tried to brush the feeling aside. Inwardly, he hoped that Virginia had not changed her mind about joining him in Kershaw now that the baby had arrived.

On Sunday afternoon, Virginia did not accompany Bill to the depot. Instead she watched him from the window as he walked up the street. Bill turned and waved one last time before he was out of sight and Virginia, holding the baby in her arms, smiled and waved a farewell from the window. A deep loneliness as never before enveloped Bill and kept company with him for days.

Work at the mine increased and Bill's time was devoted to nothing else. Because of the unsettled times, he took advantage of the extra work often working two shifts straight. The days passed swiftly and left Bill with little time to worry about Virginia and the baby.

Early on the morning of August 24th, Bill found the time to pen a letter to Virginia. He had received a letter from her the previous day and he wanted to get a reply in the mail before he started his shift at the mine.

Kershaw, South Carolina
8 a.m., Sunday
August 24th, 1936

Dear Virginia,

I certainly did enjoy a long sweet letter from you yesterday. I am glad that you and Janet are okay and I hope that you will continue to do fine because now that I have you both, I need both of you. If anything would happen to either of you, I don't know what I would do. I wish I could have stayed with you longer but you know all impossibilities.

I guess you can get all the news you want because R. L. was at Mr. Faulkenberry's Friday evening. Even if you don't want the news, get it for me. I want to straighten out a few things here.

I took out some insurance on Janet yesterday. The policy is $620.00, twenty five cents a week. That pays $85.00 the first year, *paid up policy. I can't get a receipt for it though until you come back home.*

I bought and mailed two blankets, one box of powders, two pair of booties, and one pair of rubber pants for the baby. Please excuse the twenty-five cent blanket because they didn't have but one of the others. You can give the thirty-nine cent one to Catherine if you wish.

Well, I will stop off for a while. Be good, darling. Kiss the baby for daddy and tell her hello.

So long, Dearest Pal.
Always your,
Bill

A week later, Thomas and Catherine came by for Sunday dinner with the family. Virginia gave them the thirty-nine cent blanket from Bill she had received in the mail, along with the other items he made mention of in his last letter. Catherine was pleased with the blanket and Thomas approved because it was the color blue. After dinner, they all retired to the porch to catch the cool summer breeze. The job at the power company had remained steady the past two years for Thomas insuring him and Catherine a more comfortable life than some in the predominately textile town of Clover. When the mill was short on work and stood sometimes two or three days a week, he and Catherine were happy to help her parents financially.

Although Virginia's asthma returned at times confining her to bed, she frequently walked to town to visit Mr. Oren's dime store. A new girl now filled the position Virginia once held there and Virginia enjoyed the exchange of light hearted conversations with her. When Bill sent the money to her, Virginia shopped for baby clothes and other sundries at McConnell's Department Store. Bertha and Virginia's mother were more than eager to take on the responsibility of the baby to give her some free time of her own.

Janet was a contented baby who slept throughout the night and required little attention beyond basic needs. Bertha aided in spoiling her and could often be heard crooning the familiar lullabies she once sang to the infant children she had taken into her home. Virginia's life with her parents offered her more contentment than she first thought possible.

The high temperatures of August subsided and on a perfect September morning that held only the slightest hint of fall, Virginia brought the baby to the porch to escape the confinement of the house. Janet now slept peacefully on the blankets stretched full length on the floor as several neighbors stopped by to admire her and exchange polite conversation. Mr. Parks strolled up the walk and handed a letter to Virginia. Virginia recognized Bill's familiar handwriting but remained on the porch in deep thought for a while before opening the letter. The postmark read:

Kershaw, South Carolina

3p.m.

September 2nd, 1936

Virginia opened the letter and continued to read.

Kershaw, S.C.

Wednesday night

Hello Sweetheart,

I received your letter last night and I sure was glad to hear from you. Although I am sorry my pal is having so much trouble with her asthma. I hope you don't get any worse. In fact, I hope you get well soon so that you can come home to me, honey. I need you at home, honey. The moon was full last night. I really don't believe I have seen one as beautiful as it when it was rising.

I have about four gallons of muscadine wine put up. I am planning to save two gallons for Christmas. No, honey, I am not getting drunk now. I just put that up this week. It is not ready to bottle yet.

I went to Camden Monday but I didn't get to see the man I needed to see about a job. He was in Columbia. I plan to write to him today. I don't much believe I can get the job though. I believe someone else has it. That's what I heard. I sure wish I could get it. It really is a nice place, Gin, and I believe you would like it there. I am going to do my best to get it if someone hasn't already.

I am picking muscadines and Mama is making jelly out of it for us. She was out here Sunday afternoon. Dad was with her. He was on his way to go back to Rock Hill.

Gin, please write and tell me about everything. Tell me when you want to come back home or when you can. I can't read your mind way up there. Did you get the two dollars I sent you? I will send more on Saturday. You can pay Dr. McGill some. Understand that the more I send you the longer it will be before I can see you. It will be at least two weeks now. I want to see you but I can't until I get a few debts paid. I can stay away better than I can stand to see you any other way besides okay.

Well, you will have to excuse another short letter. I had to borrow this paper. I will get a tablet today. Write soon, sweetheart. Kiss Janet for Daddy.

Always,
Your, Bill

Chapter 18

On September 14th, after a long labor, Catherine gave birth to a baby daughter. Her mother spent a week with her to help with the baby while Bertha remained with Virginia and Janet. Virginia gave witness to the pleasure that Thomas and Catherine displayed as they gazed upon the chubby, dark-haired daughter they named Colleen Ray. Virginia made a silent wish that Janet and Colleen might remain close to each other throughout their lives.

In late September, Bill rode the train from Kershaw to Clover to see the newest baby in the family and congratulate Thomas and Catherine. The time he spent with his daughter was his greatest joy and it became increasingly hard for him to part from her at weekend's end. It did not go unnoticed by Bill that the distance between him and Virginia yet remained.

"What's wrong, Virginia?" Bill asked. "I know something is. Why won't you tell me?"

"It's nothing, Bill," she answered avoiding his gaze. "I guess so much has changed in so little time that it's taking me a while to process it all."

"I think it's more than that," Bill replied. "A lot has changed and I think it's time for you and Janet to be with me in Kershaw. I can find us a place if you'll just give me an idea when you're willing to come. You both need to be with me now."

Virginia gave no reply and turned her head away from his gaze.

On Sunday evening, Bill rode the train to Kershaw alone. After all of its flurry, September quietly heralded in the arrival of October. The splendor of the month was breathtaking with its brilliant display of foliage. The air grew crisper and clearer, a welcomed relief from the record breaking temperatures of the previous summer. Virginia and Janet remained in Clover while Bill continued his work in the mine.

As often as his finances allowed, Bill traveled back and forth between Kershaw and Clover. The coolness between him and Virginia remained and in its wake left a chill that imitated the steadily declining temperatures of October. The store windows in town displayed the golden hues of fall and the smiles or frowns of jack-o-lanterns as Halloween parted the curtain for the advent of the holiday season. Virginia chose this as her favorite season of the year, the season of her birth that held the promise of Thanksgiving, Christmas, family gatherings, and holiday cheer.

Bill arrived in Clover in late November to join Virginia and Janet for Thanksgiving. Work at the mine had declined and gave Bill cause for concern. He made no mention of it as he gathered with Virginia's family for Thanksgiving dinner.

The family gathered around the table, thankful for much but most of all for the demise of this difficult year. They all clung fast to the optimism they held in the arrival of a new year. The laughter and the crackle of the fire in the hearth imparted warmth to the gathering but did little to warm the coolness between Bill and Virginia.

Virginia accompanied Bill to the depot on Sunday afternoon wearing the red coat she had purchased at McConnell's. Bill thought she looked just as lovely in it now as she had the first time he saw her in it, standing at the depot when he stepped from the train.

The last week in November, Virginia received a letter from Bill. She was hesitant to open it because she had neglected to write him as she promised and understood how disappointed he must be. The time and distance apart had taken its toll on their relationship no matter how hard Virginia pretended that it hadn't. She could not keep this from Bill much longer. She glanced at the postmark Kershaw, November 30, 1936, and opened the letter.

Kershaw, South Carolina
Sunday, A.M.

Dearest Pal,

I am writing to ask you to please answer one of the letters I wrote you. What's wrong, Virginia? Are you sick or have you been sick? What about the promise you made to me that you would write and not do this way? It has been one week and one day today since I saw you and I haven't heard a word from you yet. I hope you haven't been sick, darling. I am worried about you and Janet, honey. It's not right for you to do me this way. It is lonesome here and when you don't write it just makes it worse.

I am at the house now. I stay right here by myself when I am not working.

Have you been watching the moon, honey? It was full last night. It sure was beautiful and has been for the past three nights. I wish we had a place to stay that was suitable to live in so you and Janet could be with me. I miss you and Janet a lot. It won't be long though, I hope. One week of it has gone by already. I don't know whether I will be able to get a house or not. We may have to take rooms with someone. I asked about a house in town yesterday. The fellow told me that his houses were full. He said that there had been about six families wanting a house from him in the past week. We can do some way. I suppose.

Darling, I will give you your permanent for your hair for Christmas anytime you want to get it. Just let me know and I will send you the money. I thought I would tell you so that if you want to get it before Christmas, let me know. They will be pretty busy around Christmas you know. Let me know how much it will be.

I am sending you a stamped envelope. I bought three stamps yesterday and forgot about yours until I put it on the envelope. I want to hear from you soon too. Tell me what the trouble is if there is any. Be good, darling, and please write to me.

Kiss sweet Janet for me. Tell her that Santa Claus will see her Christmas, if not before.

So long, Dearest Pal. You be good, darling, and please write to me. I would write more but I am saving some for seed. Don't be worrying your sweet self to death, sweetheart, because I love you. That's enough isn't it?

Always,
Your, Bill

P.S. Please send my mail to R.S.'s. I had it changed so that I can get it sooner.

Part v
The Parting

Chapter 19

Virginia held her coat tight against her small frame as she walked in the chilly December air. The clouds in the sky held the promise of snow and a clear chance for a white Christmas.

At the end of November, Virginia had reclaimed her job at Mr. Oren's. Although she found it difficult to leave the baby, she had confidence in her mother and Bertha to attend to the Janet's every need. Bill sent money to her on a regular basis but with the added income she earned at Mr. Oren's she hoped to ease the strain she and Bill found themselves under. Virginia wrote Bill less and less these days and Bill grew increasingly weary of the situation. He continued to write, though not as often, and held to his plans to spend Christmas in Clover with Virginia and the baby. All mention for Virginia and Janet to join him in Kershaw, dropped without notice, from any correspondence with her. Bill accepted the fact that at this time she was not receptive to the idea. No use to beat a dead horse. But Bill refused to relinquish the tiny glimmer of hope in his heart that in time she would change her mind.

Not long after Virginia received her last letter from Bill, she received another package from him that contained gifts for Janet for Christmas. Bill had included in the package a brief note that read

December 15th, 1936

Dearest Pal,

Things are okay here. Hope they are in Clover. I will be arriving there on Friday the 23rd at four o'clock. Please put the enclosed items underneath the tree for Janet.

Guess by now you have received the money I sent to get your hair done for Christmas and that by now you have taken care of that. It's anybody's guess what the New Year might hold for us here at the mine. As of now, I am working steadily though not as many hours. Kiss Janet for me and if possible meet me at the depot on the 23rd.

Always,
Your, Bill

Virginia left Mr. Oren's store an hour early on the 23rd to meet Bill at the depot. The train arrived on schedule at four o'clock and when Bill emerged Virginia greeted him with a warm hug. They walked the short distance to her parents' home hand in hand.

Virginia and Bill had little time together with all the added household preparations for Christmas. Bill visited with Thomas and Catherine to remove himself from the fray and later dropped by to visit Daniel and Anna Jane. On his way back from Daniel's, Bill lingered in town for a while. He soaked in the atmosphere of Christmas, unique to small textile towns this time of year. He walked in the reflection of the multicolored lights that Thomas and his fellow workers had strung high across the road from one side of the street to another. He lazily strolled down the street and gazed into each store window. He embraced all the sounds and sights of Christmas and took time to have a conversation with the Santa on the street corner. He took it all in as if he might never come this way again.

When Bill arrived home, the packages were wrapped and lay resting underneath the tree. The fire in the hearth crackled and popped while Janet slept an infant's peaceful sleep in her crib nearby.

"What a perfect scene," Bill thought, as he sat before the fire.

Christmas morning broke cold and cloudy. Sounds emanating from the kitchen bore evidence of a Christmas dinner in progress.

Twelve o'clock found everyone seated around the table. Virginia's Aunt Erline and Uncle Erwin joined them accompanied by their young daughter, Daisy, and their son James. Thomas and Catherine, along with their infant daughter, Colleen, had arrived much earlier. While Catherine busied herself in the kitchen, Thomas and Bill took the opportunity for a private conversation in another room. Thomas was an avid hunter, something Bill knew very little about, but he found the stories that Thomas recounted on the subject somewhat entertaining.

Virginia had chosen Christmas Day, her birthday, for the baptism of their daughter. In mid afternoon, after the Christmas gifts were opened and dinner complete, they traveled down the winding dirt road to the small Methodist church where Bill first met Virginia. As they pulled up to the church , Bill could almost see her there sitting under the oak tree, her dark hair shining, in vivid contrast to the white camellia pinned behind her ear.

Snuggled in a white blanket, her chubby legs kicking underneath a white christening dress, Janet Leanne Blackmon received the rite of baptism. The glow of pride on Bill and Virginia's face gave stiff competition to the mellow glow of the candle lit church.

As the small sprinkling of family members exited the warm comfort of the cozy church, a light dusting of snow began to fall.

"A white Christmas after all," Bill commented.

"Just what we wanted," Virginia replied.

Bill and Virginia stood in the snow and bid each family member farewell. When Virginia turned away, Bill remained with the snow falling around his shoulders and watched until they all disappeared from sight.

Tuesday afternoon, Bill returned to Kershaw. He found it more difficult with each parting to leave his wife and daughter behind and returned several times to the crib in front of the fire to leave soft kisses on Janet's cheeks. Virginia had gone to work earlier that morning and Bill dropped by Mr. Oren's to say good-bye to her on his way to the depot. He made no mention of her joining him in Kershaw.

Nineteen thirty-seven slipped in on eagles' wings of optimism. The difficult years of the depression began to fade away with time, only to be recounted best by those who bore witness to it, passing down their account from one generation to the next.

The letters from Bill to Virginia ceased to arrive after that snowy Christmas day in 1936. Her attempts to contact Bill came to no avail. Daniel made several trips to Kershaw to find his old friend only to learn each time that Bill had not resurfaced.

In time, Virginia accepted Bill's absence and the mystery that surrounded it.

Part v1
Conclusion

The loud thud as the car door slammed jolted Janet into the present and drew her attention away from the letters. In haste, she returned them to the antique box and locked the lid.

Throughout her lifetime, Janet continued to experience compelling moments that bid her return to the letters. But for now, she chose to keep them locked away forever a part of the past.

The End

Epilogue

It is not known whether Bill ever returned to Clover before Virginia's death fourteen years later. It is known that Virginia never remarried and continued to raise her daughter in the home of her parents. She now rests peacefully at Woodside Cemetery in Clover, South Carolina. However, it is recorded in the family history that Bill also rests at Woodside in an unmarked grave. Perhaps he has found peace beside Virginia next to the marker inscribed

Virginia Dare Nivens
Wife of B. C. Blackmon
"Dearest Pal"

Printed in the United States
132475LV00007B/145/P

9 781438 908670